PRAISE FOR DAEDALUS FILES

A strange thing happened to me while reading Robert G. Williscroft's *The Daedalus Files*: I felt it hard to believe it was fiction. Earlier, I had read his novel *Slingshot* about the world's first Space Launch Loop, and since *The Daedalus Files* follows it, I should have known it was fiction. Still, this hard science-fiction tale is told with such vivid, realistic, sometimes visceral detail and moment-by-moment suspense that I almost completely lost myself in it.

Daedalus LEO is even more exciting than *Daedalus*, the first story in this book with more thrills, more near-escapes, more humor, and more spectacular sightseeing of the Earth far below. More romance too, for that matter. This time around the author has upped the ante. It's the first manned LEO (Low Earth Orbit) drop, and instead of 80 klicks, the *Gryphon 10* has to drop 160, or twice as far.

Daedalus Squad brilliantly advances the Gryphon missions. This time, a six-man squad in improved wingsuits launches into Low Earth Orbit and travels around the globe before landing. Its purpose is to do it eventually under combat conditions. As you might expect, something is bound to go wrong with this training mission, and it does, leading to a tense conclusion.

The near-future scientific and technological detail here is thoroughly convincing. As in the author's previous stories, maps show the global paths of the men and make it easy to follow their progress in space. At times, you even feel you're along for the ride.

Daedalus Combat is a fitting conclusion to and culmination of the other three stories in this action-packed, hard science-fiction book. When Pirates snatch a U.S. Senator and probable next President from a ship and hold him for one hundred million dollars ransom, the Navy SEALS quickly move to rescue him. Once again Derek "Tiger" Baily's six-man SWIC squad is featured, only this time, the operation is "dramatically different from anything any warrior had ever done before." Why? Because it's the first time anyone has ever "dropped from LEO into a combat scenario."

It's the full nature of this combat scenario that is the real "Wow" factor here. All the different units of the military machine must work together if the mission is to succeed. The action and suspense are intense, and they kept me turning the pages until the very end.

— Professor John B. Rosenman, Norfolk State University
Former Chairman of the Board, Horror Writers Association
Author of *The Inspector of the Cross Series*

Afraid of Heights?

Then you won't make it as a member of SEALS Winged Insertion Command.

For a once in a lifetime thrill, follow the thoughts and actions of Derek "Tiger" Baily, most adept member of Second Platoon, First Squad as he wrings out the details of making a wingsuit jump from a platform eighty kilometers (fifty miles) above Jarvis Island on the Equator in the middle of the Pacific Ocean. Tiger Baily reached that platform using the "Slingshot" space portal system described in Robert G. Williscroft's richly detailed series of hard science fiction novels, *The Starchild Trilogy*. But rather than launch into space from the Fred Noonan Skyport, Tiger Baily attempts a 236-mile traverse over the ever-threatening and oh-so-deep ocean waters. This is what SEALs do, test new means of surreptitiously inserting themselves into combat zones.

While the beginning and middle of Williscroft's short story are mesmerizing, the fifty-mile high drop and long-distance transit will have you holding your breath.

Much to Williscroft's credit, the physics and dynamics of Tiger's record-breaking flight seem spot on.

Daedalus LEO is about the unimaginable, yet somehow, Robert Williscroft not only imagined it but made it real—and breathtakingly thrilling.

The idea of a human being deliberately placing himself in low earth orbit to carry out a proof of concept mission is an image as fresh, and yet disturbing, as they come. Mind you, Derek "Tiger" Baily is an extraordinary human, and this is no ordinary story. Those of us growing up in the space age know full well that reentry from orbit is terrifyingly dangerous. The fires of reentry consume foolish mortals who make the slightest mistake. And mistakes and problems arise aplenty in Tiger's trial run.

In *Daedalus Squad*, a SEALS Winged Insertion Command (SWIC) squad drops from Low Earth Orbit.

The technology for getting there was well explained in Williscroft's previous novel, *Slingshot*. *The Daedalus Files* concern the development of special combat operations with easy access to space.

As with most experimental research, there are challenges—and mishaps galore. In this storyline, with humans hurtling around the Earth at orbital velocities, there is precious little room for error. Controlled re-entry of a human body is even riskier. All of that riskiness translates into an exciting read.

Aside from the thrills inherent in such feats of heroism, this story is educational. If you've wondered how orbiting spacecraft maneuver to change orbits, or rendezvous with other orbiting bodies (in this story, literally human bodies), *Daedalus Squad* will reveal enough of the lingo to help you search online and find out how it's done. That education alone adds an unexpected dimension to this treasure of a story.

Clandestine military operations depend on the element of surprise: Navy SEALS fast-roping from a helicopter, or exiting a submarine in the middle of the night. But the ultimate surprise would be dropping a combat team on an unsuspecting enemy from low earth orbit (LEO). Not LEO of a spaceship, or spaceplane, but of actual combatants, living, breathing human beings, armed to the teeth, crossing oceans in minutes, and pouncing as a team of flying, fire-breathing dragons.

Who would have thought?

Well, that's exactly the point. No one would…except Navy SEAL "Tiger" Bailey, Commanding Officer of SEALS Winged Insertion Command Three (SWIC-3).

Robert Williscroft places you inside the action, inside the incredible space launches, the orbital rendezvous, the almost flaming reentry, the on-the-fly change of plans, attack under hellacious conditions, and egress from the combat scene.

Like any combat operation, there are risks at every step of the way, and Williscroft brings you, the reader, along for the ride of a lifetime.

At the end of these three short reads, you'll breathe a sigh of relief, let out a little cheer for our unsung heroes, and then wonder—could this really happen?

Don't ask this reviewer. I'm sworn to secrecy.

— Dr. John R. Clarke
Author of *The Jason Parker Series*

Williscroft's usual attention to technical detail and firsthand experience with military ops pays off in these wild tales set in the world of his *Slingshot*, about the first wingsuit jump from a launch loop, then from LEO, followed by a squad of jumpers, and finally, their jump into live combat.

The idea of jumping from orbit using little more than a spacesuit and a re-entry pack goes back at least to Heinlein's *Starship Troopers*, and I've used it myself, but Williscroft puts a new twist on it as Navy SEAL "Tiger" Baily makes the jump first from 80 km and then LEO. A great tale, with his usual attention to detail.

"Tiger" Baily, the wingsuited, space-jumping hero of Williscroft's *Daedalus Files*, has the stakes upped once again as his whole team makes a jump from orbit. This time they're leaving nothing to chance and have already simulated every possible bad-news scenario they can think of. Too bad nature can come up with something they didn't think of. Another fun ride, if your idea of fun includes death-defying action.

The test and training runs are over; now it's time for the SWIC to see real action. Williscroft's final tale in this book, *Daedalus Combat*, literally starts with a bang and keeps on going...

— Alastair Mayer
Author of *The T-Space Series*

The Daedalus Files are four science fiction short stories that blend the boundaries of fact and fiction as seamlessly as the late master, Michael Crichton. They're the type of story that leaves you asking questions and discussing with your coworkers in the break room. The stories are told by Derek "Tiger" Baily, a member of an elite SEALS team.

In *Daedalus*, he completes the first jump in an experimental wingsuit from a skyport 80 km above the Earth. Now, if you've read *Slingshot*, a full-length sci-fi thriller published by Williscroft a few years ago (see my review—5 stars for this well-crafted and thought-provoking story) you'll know all about the skyport, a marvel of engineering that could be close to being realized (really!). And if you haven't read *Slingshot*, no worries because an excerpt is thoughtfully included at the end of *The Daedalus Files*.

Tiger is a self-professed adrenalin junky who doesn't shy away from a challenge. I won't share any spoilers here, because it is best to allow yourself to become one with Tiger as he flies his wingsuit to his target landing zone—a tiny atoll in the Pacific Ocean. What begins as a normal drop soon turns into a terrifying descent into Nature's fury that will leave you in a cold sweat.

Daedalus LEO chronicles Lt. Commander Derek "Tiger" Baily's flight from low-Earth orbit in a wingsuit. To call the Gryphon-10 a wingsuit is a stretch, but I think it conveys the idea without introducing spoilers. As with all of Williscroft's work, the writing is tight and realistic. The characters are three-dimensional against a backdrop of excitement, thrills, and cliff-hangers. And the science in this sci-fi is damn accurate. In fact, much of the plot and details are science fact, and part of the fun, as with the work of the late great Michael Crichton, is trying to discern the thin line between truth and fiction.

Daedalus Squad continues the adventures of Lt.Cdr. Derek "Tiger" Baily. Sporting the newest version of the wingsuit (the Gryphon 10 Mk 4), Tiger plans to link up with the other members of his squad in Low Earth Orbit and then descend in formation to a landing at the Amargosa Valley. When the plan goes awry, Tiger must think quickly and use his considerable flying skills to avoid certain death.

Daedalus Combat brings "Tiger" Baily into a rescue mission with no margin for error. Sporting the newest version of the fully-armed wingsuit (the Gryphon 10 Mk 4), Tiger and his squad must rescue a U.S. Senator—and presumed future President—who is being held for ransom by pirates. Williscroft demonstrates his knowledge of military tactics and equipment to paint an all-too-realistic picture of what could be tomorrow's headlines.

Each of *The Daedalus Files* adventures, told through the voice of Tiger, is a short story, and I'd encourage fans of sci-fi and military thrillers to read them in order since they stitch together smoothly into a comprehensive tale of adventure and suspense. Together, they are an exciting, hard-charging read that is sure to satisfy thriller and sci-fi readers.

— **Dr. Dave Edlund**
USA Today **Bestselling Author –**
The Peter Savage Thrillers

THE DAEDALUS FILES

SEALS Winged Insertion Command (SWIC)

THE DAEDALUS FILES

SEALS Winged Insertion Command (SWIC)

by

Robert G. Williscroft

Fresh Ink Group
Guntersville

THE DAEDALUS FILES
SEALS Winged Insertion Command (SWIC)

Copyright © 2020
by Robert G. Williscroft
All rights reserved

Fresh Ink Group
An Imprint of:
The Fresh Ink Group, LLC
Box 931
Guntersville, AL 35976
info@FreshInkGroup.com
FreshInkGroup.com

Edition 1.0 2020

Cover art by Anik / FIG
Artwork by Robert G. Williscroft
Book design by Amit Dey / FIG
Covers by Stephen Geez / FIG

Names, characters, and incidents in this story are either products of the author's imagination or are used fictitiously. Any resemblance to actual events, locations, names, and people, living or dead, is entirely coincidental and beyond the intent of the author and publisher.

Except as permitted under the U.S. Copyright Act of 1976 and except for brief quotations in critical reviews or articles, no portion of this book's content may be stored in any medium, transmitted in any form, used in whole or part, or sourced for derivative works such as videos, television, and motion pictures, without prior written permission from the publisher.

BISAC Subject Headings:
F1CO28020 FICTION / Science Fiction / Hard Science Fiction
FIC002000 FICTION / Action & Adventure
F1CO2801 0 FICTION / Science Fiction / Action & Adventure

ISBN-13: 978-1-947867-87-1 Papercover
ISBN-13: 978-1-947867-88-8 Hardcover
ISBN-13: 978-1-947867-89-5 Ebooks

Library of Congress Control Number: 2020903624

DEDICATION

These four stories are dedicated to parachute record-holder Alan Eustace, to Wingsuit Flyers Dean Potter and Graham Hunt, and to the World Wingsuit community. They are also dedicated to all of the Teams, all of the U.S. Navy SEALS, who put our safety ahead of theirs world-wide.

TABLE OF CONTENTS

Acknowledgments xix
Foreword xxi
Cast Of Characters xxv
Chapter One—Daedalus 1
    California—Several Years In The Past 1
    Yosemite Park—Two Years Later 1
    Coronado, California—The Gryphon 2
    Coronado, California—Gryphon Drops 4
    Equatorial Pacific—Slingshot 6
        Figure 1—The Slingshot Space Launch Loop 6
    Equatorial Pacific—Howland Island 7
    Equatorial Pacific—Baker Island 8
    Equatorial Pacific—Fred Noonan Skyport (Jarvis Island) 10
    Equatorial Pacific—Gryphon Flight 12
        Figure 2—Howland, Baker, Jarvis & Kiribati Islands—
        Flight of the Gryphon 13
    Kiritimati Island 17
        Figure 3—Kiritimati Island –Gryphon splashdown 18
    Daedalus—Finale 20

Chapter Two—Daedalus Leo 23
   *Figure 4—Gryphon and pallet with Tiger Baily in leo in an
      uncontrolled tumble.* 23
   Low Earth Orbit 23
   Coronado—San Diego—Several Days Earlier. 24
   Coronado—Gryphon-10 25
   Coronado—Max 26
   Slingshot—Equatorial Pacific 27
   LEO—Unmanned Drop. 27
   Coronado—Manned Drop Prep 28
   Howland & Baker Islands—Prelaunch 28
   Amelia Earhart Skyport—Prelaunch 31
   *Figure 5—Gryphon and pallet on the fred noonanskyport
      platform ready to receive a rider.* 33
   Amelia Earhart Skyport—Launch 34
   Slingshot Rail—Coupled 35
   Figure 6—Gryphon and pallet with tiger baily approaching LEO. ... 36
   LEO—Manned 36
   LEO—Disaster 38
   LEO—Rendezvous 41
   LEO—Miss. 42
   *Figure 7—Spare Gryphon on pallet with oxygen tanks and
      makeshift piping.* 44
   LEO—Orbit Shift 45
   *Figure 8—Orbital paths as they pass over the u.s. and Mexico
      of the original orbit, the resulting orbit after the accident,
      and the final orbit following the correction.* 48

Figure 9—Orbital paths from Kinshasa to Australia of the original orbit, the resulting orbit after the accident, and the final orbit following the correction. 48

Figure 10—Orbital paths over the Pacific of the original orbit, the resulting orbit after the accident, and the final orbit following the correction over the Pacific. 49

LEO—Manned Drop 49

Houston Flight Control—Landing 52

Figure 11—Gryphon with Tiger Baily about to crash into an unaware bike rider. 53

Daedalus Leo—Finale 53

Chapter Three—Daedalus Squad 57

8,000 Meters Above Death Valley 57

Coronado—San Diego—Several Days Earlier 57

Coronado—Gryphon-10, Mk 4 58

Coronado—Max 59

Coronado—Squad Drop Prep 60

Howland & Baker Islands—Prelaunch 60

Amelia Earhart Skyport—Prelaunch 62

Amelia Earhart Skyport—Launch 65

Slingshot Rail 65

Figure 12—Slingshot Space Launch Loop with the Hohmann Transfer Orbit and the last leg of the final orbit track from Australia to the final landing at Amargosa Valley. 66

LEO 66

Figure 13—Hohmann Transfer Orbit to the apogee over Lagos. Final circularized orbit track from apogee. 68

Figure 14— Tiger Baily's SWIC team on pallets in LEO with spare oxygen and fuel tanks. 69

LEO—Squad Drop 69

Figure 15—Final orbit track over the Indian Ocean to Australia. ... 70

Figure 16—Tiger Baily's SWIC Team in formation in LEO preparing to drop. 72

Death Valley—Bird Strike 73

Death Valley Snag 74

Figure 17—C-130 Hercules aircraft receiving Tiger Baily's damaged Gryphon with assistance from Jerico. 75

Daedalus Squad—Finale 77

Chapter Four—Daedalus Combat 81

Mozambique Channel—200 Kilometers Northeast of Mayotte Island 81

Amelia Earhart Skyport—Prelaunch. 83

Amelia Earhart Skyport—Launch 85

Slingshot Rail 86

Figure 18—Slingshot Space Launch Loop with the Hohmann Transfer Orbit. 87

LEO. 87

Figure 19—Tiger Baily's SWIC team in LEO Preparing For Drop. ... 88

LEO—COMBAT DROP 89

Figure 20—The Hohmann Transfer Orbit and the apogee with the shortened LEO path. the drop point and destination, Mayotte Island. 90

Figure 21—Rog and his team head to free CS Platypus. Tiger and Jerico on their way to rescue Senator Manfred. 92

MAYOTTE ISLAND—*CS PLATYPUS* 93
   Figure 22—Mayotte Island with Port of Longoni and
      Doujani Reservoir 94
MAYOTTE ISLAND—DOUJANI RESERVOIR 95
DOUJANI RESERVOIR SNAG 97
   Figure 23—The Fulton ground-to-air extraction system 98
MAYOTTE ISLAND—LAGOON 99
DAEDALUS COMBAT—FINALE 100
PLEASE POST A REVIEW FOR THE DAEDALUS FILES 102
Excerpt From The First Chapter Of: SLINGSHOT 103
WORDS OF PRAISE FOR SLINGSHOT 112
ABOUT THE AUTHOR 115
OTHER WORKS BY ROBERT WILLISCROFT 119
CONNECT WITH ROBERT WILLISCROFT 121
THE DAEDALUS FILES GLOSSARY 123

ACKNOWLEDGMENTS

Several people contributed to the creation of this book.

Most significantly, my wonderful wife, Jill, whom I first met when I returned from a year at the South Pole conducting atmospheric research, and who finally consented to marry me nearly thirty years later, pored over these stories with her discerning engineer's eye. She kept my timeline honest, and made sure that regular readers could understand fully the arcane details of the Launch Loop and the Gryphon.

Jill's twin sons, Arthur and Robert, also read the manuscript and provided their insights.

Hard science fiction authors Alastair Mayer, and Profs. John Rosenman and John Cark, and USA Today bestselling author Dave Edlund reviewed the manuscript and offered their editorial insights.

It goes without saying that any remaining omissions, errors, and mistakes fall directly on my shoulders.

Robert G. Williscroft, PhD
Centennial, Colorado
February 2020

FOREWORD

Slingshot is my novel about constructing the world's first Space Launch Loop. The inventor of the concept, Keith Lofstrom, wrote the foreword to that novel. Here is a portion of that Foreword.

Imagine a stream of water out of a fire hose. Without air friction, the stream might make a parabolic arc 20 meters high. Faster, and the arc goes higher and farther. A stream moving 7.3 kilometers per second would come down on the other side of the planet, and a stream moving 11 kilometers per second would keep going into interplanetary space. Wrap the stream in a frictionless hose, and...THAT won't work either. But what if...?

The launch loop: REPLACE the water with flexible iron pipe, 5 centimeters outer diameter, 3 metric tons per kilometer, moving at 14 kilometers per second. Bend it to the curvature of the earth with a stationary magnetic track, 7 metric tons per kilometer, 2,000 kilometers long, at 80 kilometers altitude. Stabilize the moving iron with electromagnets controlled by fast electronics. Turn it around at the ends with powerful magnets, and complete the loop.

On the eastbound section, 5-metric-ton payloads ride on magnets designed for high drag, which accelerates payloads at 3 gees. Payloads exit the east end of the track between 7.7 and 11 kilometers per second, to equatorial low earth orbits, to the moon, or to interplanetary space. Launching a payload weighing 5 metric tons to low earth orbit consumes 180 megawatt-hours, about $15,000 worth of electricity, or $3 per kilogram of payload. Passengers will still need vehicles and air, but freight can be launched on wooden shipping pallets. This small launch loop can launch 2,000 5-metric-ton payloads to orbit per day. Heavier launch loops can launch thousands of standard 30-metric-ton intermodal shipping containers per hour. They can also store peak power for the global electrical grid. Space travel can be as cheap as ocean cargo travel.

In the early 1980s, I published in an *American Astronautical Society Newsletter* and other journals, and presented at many conferences. In England, physicist Paul Birch wrote about orbital rings in the *Journal of the British Interplanetary Society*. Ken Brakke, a math professor in Pennsylvania, published his version of orbital rings.

Ken, Paul, and I met at one of the Space Studies Institute conferences at Princeton. We spent three days developing nomenclature, doing math, finding errors and fixes. I met Robert Williscroft in the mid-1990s in Philadelphia while I was on a trip to the East Coast. He had contacted me about a novel he was outlining—*Slingshot*. We spent a day together becoming acquainted, and have kept in touch since then. *Slingshot* in its current form is a result of our brainstorming during that visit.

For years afterward, Paul and I swapped ideas. Under Jerome Pearson's leadership, and with our friend John Knapman, we submitted grant proposals until Paul's untimely passing in 2012. We were friends, never competitors, though Paul was much better at reciting Tennyson. I hope one of us will be the first launch loop astronaut. Conflict makes great stories, but friendship makes great lives, so I now pass page control to my friend R.G....

So there you have it. I wrote *Slingshot*. It was launched at the International Space Elevator Conference in Seattle in August 2015, and the book resides on the desk of every Space Elevator scientist in the world. Space Launch Loops appear in the subsequent books in *The Starchild Trilogy*, and anyone familiar with my *Trilogy* knows all about these commercial space launch systems.

When I discovered the *Gryphon* rigid wingsuit, the four-part story you are about to read pushed itself into my consciousness. The *Gryphon* is a perfect accouterment to U.S. Navy SEALS operations. Chapter one is the natural consequence of Slingshot's skyports effectively being 80 km tall towers. Chapter two takes it to the next logical level—Low Earth Orbit (LEO). Chapter three brings an entire SEALS squad into the action, and chapter four drops the SEALS squad from LEO into live-action.

I challenge you to find the fine line between reality and fiction in these stories.

Robert G. Williscroft
Centennial, Colorado
February 2020

CAST OF CHARACTERS

For Chapter One:

SEAL Winged Insertion Command Three (SWIC-3)

Lt. Brad Nelson—Officer-in-Charge of Second Platoon.
Lt. Tom Spitzer—Executive Officer Second Platoon.
Senior Chief Jerry Boldt—In charge of Second Platoon, First Squad.
Derek "Tiger" Baily—Narrator, member of Second Platoon, First Squad.

Launch Loop International (LLI)

Apryl Searson—Diver EMT.

For Chapters Two through Four:

SEAL Winged Insertion Command (SWIC)

Navy Capt. Brad Nelson—Commanding Officer SWIC.
Lt.Cdr. Tom Spitzer—Executive Officer SWIC.
Mother—Controlling computer synchronized across each unit in an operation.
Max—Full-size *Gryphon-10* simulator

SEAL Winged Insertion Command Three (SWIC-3)

Lt.Cdr. Derek "Tiger" Baily—Narrator, Commanding Officer SWIC-3.
Jim Fox—Executive Officer SWIC-3.
Master Chief Jerry Boldt—Master Chief SWIC-3.
Senior Chief Bob Baxter—Master Chief Boldt's second.

1st Squad—SWIC-3 (Chapters 2-4)

Navy Lt. Roger "Rog" Brook—Squad Leader
Chief Douglas Slade
Petty Officer 1st Class Francisco "Jerico" Rodriguez
Petty Officer 1st Class Ronald "Cappy" Caplan
Petty Officer 2nd Class Peter "Pete" Farwall
Not participating in the drop
Petty Officer 2nd Class Benjamin "Benny" Williams
Petty Officer 2nd Class Christopher "Piggy" Pigwell
Petty Officer 3rd Class Clyde "Cowboy" Horseman

Launch Loop International (LLI)

Sam Davidson—Slingshot Director.
Apryl Searson—Chief Diver EMT.

U.S. Air Force C-130 Hercules

Lt.Col. Randal Dorsey, U.S. Air Force—C-130 Hercules pilot
U.S. Navy Aircraft Carrier Fighter Squadron
Lt. Joe "Happy" Snider—U.S. Navy fighter pilot
Lt. Bob "Borax" Johnson—U.S. Navy fighter pilot

Tasmanian Ocean Cruises

Capt. Mansur Darusman—Captain of the *CS Platypus*
Senator Jack Manfred—Wealthy scion of the American East Coast Manfred political family. Personal friend of the President and likely to be the next U.S. President.

DAEDALUS
SWIC Basejump from Fred Noonan Skyport

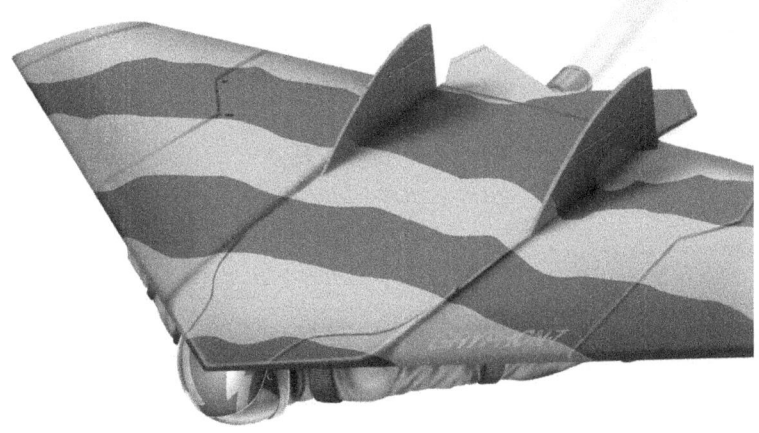

Chapter One

CHAPTER ONE

DAEDALUS

CALIFORNIA—SEVERAL YEARS IN THE PAST

Obviously, I survived, since I am telling this story. But it's not that simple—let me explain.

My name is Derek Baily. I'm an extreme sports enthusiast, an adrenaline junkie. It all started several years ago when I made my first parachute jump. Before that, I was just your typical skateboarder, snowboarder, trick-bike rider…I think you get the idea. I had gone parasailing a couple of times, and it was really cool. I decided I wanted to do more of that and was talking it over with my buds. That's when one of them suggested that I try a jump.

"Jump out of a perfectly safe airplane?" I asked, but only half in jest.

"How about next Saturday?" he said.

YOSEMITE PARK—TWO YEARS LATER

One thing led to another, and a couple of years later, on May 16, I found myself standing on Taft Point in Yosemite National Park, dressed in a fire-engine-red wingsuit. It wasn't as if I had permission or anything, it was just something I had to do. I was there to commemorate the ill-fated flight of Dean Potter and Graham Hunt from the same spot on the same day back in 2015. A couple of Forest Rangers with a bullhorn did their very best to stop me. They had followed me to the Point, and were perhaps three meters away, and I still wasn't quite ready—I mean, I still had to narrow my focus. But it was then or never, so I jumped.

The first hundred meters were a bit rough as I got my act together. I would have flipped off the Rangers, but my hands were kinda full. My wingsuit was significantly better than was Potter's. He had a three-to-one glide ratio—better than most, but not quite good enough to hit the slot that loomed ahead of me. It could have been a down-draft that got him and Hunt, but I think they cut it a bit too close. I had a glide ratio of five-to-one, which meant hitting the slot was a piece of cake. I cleared it by about a meter-and-a-half, with clear flying beyond. I stretched it out as long as possible, and finally popped my canopy as close to the ground as I dared—maybe a hundred meters or so. I landed standing, soft as a feather. By the time the Rangers got there, my pickup crew and I were long gone.

Like I said, that's how I got from there to here.

CORONADO, CALIFORNIA—THE GRYPHON

The worldwide wingsuit community is quite small, although it has grown in the last few decades. Even so, there were less than a thousand of us—that is until the military figured out how to turn our sport into a pretty nifty weapon system with a little help from the Special Parachute and Logistics Consortium (SPELCO) in Germany. SPELCO had built an experimental wingsuit called the *Gryphon* that, in its original version, had a glide ratio of five-to-one—when everything else was between two-and-a-half and three to one. It was pretty exciting, except no one could afford one. It turned out the Navy SEAL Teams picked up on the concept, and quietly developed a combat model.

Someone in the SEAL hierarchy concluded it might be useful to recruit guys from the wingsuit community. They even put together a special program that bypassed regular boot camp and all the other stuff a guy normally goes through before being assigned to BUDS—Basic Underwater Demolition/SEAL training. About a year after I shot the slot in Yosemite, I found myself in Coronado, California, training with a bunch of the toughest bad-asses I had ever met. BUDS was the hardest thing I ever did, literally, absolutely! Somehow I made it through. Don't ask me how I did it, because

I don't have a clue. I just put one foot in front of the other, raised my arms for one more stroke in the surf, dug down and found another push-up…I just slogged along, firmly believing I was sucking hind tit, barely surviving, hoping against hope that I would make it through.

As it turned out, to my total astonishment, I was one of the top guys in my class. Beyond BUDS, I went through a whole series of advanced training scenarios. Even though I had been recruited specifically for my wingsuit background, the SEALs insisted that I undergo the entire training cycle. Two years later—yeah, that's right, a full two years later—I finally reported to my new outfit, the SEAL Winged Insertion Command, SWIC for short.

SWIC was a team unto itself, filling a new slot in the Naval Special Warfare Group Five hierarchy. It consisted of three teams. SWIC-1 covered the Pacific and Middle East, SWIC-2 covered Europe, the Med, and Africa, and SWIC-3 covered worldwide. SWIC-1 and 3 were based in Coronado, and SWIC-2 was in Norfolk. I was assigned to Second Platoon in SWIC-3. Lt. Brad Nelson was in charge, and his second was Lt. Tom Spitzer. I was in First Squad run by Senior Chief Jerry Boldt. My platoon was working closely with SPELCO developing the latest incarnation of the *Gryphon*.

The *Gryphon* was a one-man unit that enabled a person to "fly," the only thing it still had in common with the wingsuits I had flown. The old wingsuits were really nothing more than a suit with fabric filling the gaps between stretched out arms and ankles, and between the legs. The *Gryphon* was a carapace that you strapped on your body. It stopped short of your feet, but in flight could extend to a full two meters, stretching beyond your feet. It attached to the legs and arms, with special controls for each hand, and had a broad Velcro band across the midriff. It had extensible delta wings with a three-meter wingspan. The back end contained a small steerable hypergolic rocket engine, and the left and right wings each contained pressurized hypergolic fuel components. Switches in the hand units controlled the fuel valves. The *Gryphon* had a heads-up display with height-over-ground, airspeed, groundspeed, compass, and GPS coordinates superimposed on a map, plus various system readouts.

Here is the really amazing thing about these suckers. When I flew my old wingsuits, I had to pop a chute at about 300 meters, certainly no less than 100, because their typical airspeed was between 180 and 260 kilometers per hour that I needed to shed before landing. When flying a *Gryphon*, I can land with the same light touch I get from my best sport parachute.

CORONADO, CALIFORNIA—GRYPHON DROPS

Lt. Nelson had us make hundreds of drops from aircraft, coming in for soft landings. After each drop, under Nelson's close supervision, we would adjust this, change that, and then see how the modifications worked in another drop. Every now and again, one of us would have to deploy his emergency chute, because a particular modification screwed things up. Nelson was cool when this happened, but we could tell that his concern skyrocketed. Generally, however, we improved with every drop, much to the lieutenant's satisfaction. In a static drop, the *Gryphon* had a glide ratio of ten-to-one. That meant we could deploy at 3,000 meters and land thirty klicks away—soundlessly. Without fuel, the *Gryphon* could be collapsed and rolled into a one-and-a-half-meter-long roll that weighed just a few kilos and could be stowed easily, or even carried across the back. With fuel, if you still had some left after landing, it was just a bit bulkier, but still eminently man-transportable.

With the hypergolic rocket and full tanks, the *Gryphon* could fly horizontally for thirty klicks. A standing launch from the ground used up about a klick of fuel, but a launch from any height over ten meters gave you the full thirty. Climbing consumed fuel quickly, but a powered drop extended the horizontal range by thirty klicks.

With Lt. Nelson mother-henning us all the way, we worked our way up to a 10,000-meter drop, carrying oxygen, of course. To put things into perspective, that's about 1,200 meters higher than Mt. Everest. Once we were comfortable doing this (but don't kid yourself, it never got routine), we set up for a 15,000-meter drop—from a balloon. Everyone in my squad volunteered, but I got chosen, probably because of my extensive prior wingsuit experience.

I'm not going to spend a lot of your time with the details of that drop. The thinner air in the initial minutes dropped my glide ratio way down, so I compensated with the rocket to generate some significant forward motion. When my groundspeed reached about 200, I secured the motor and shortly found enough air to regain my ten-to-one. Basically, that was it. I landed nearly 150 klicks away without further rocket use. Since I had a bit of trouble determining my rate of descent, we added a descent-rate meter to the heads-up display for follow-on drops to what now was the *Gryphon (Mk 7-Mod 1)*—or just *Gryphon-7* for short. After that, Nelson let each squad member make the balloon drop, all without incident.

I know you have never heard of any of this, but you have to understand that this was all top-secret stuff. We were developing ways to drop into an enemy's presence with total surprise, take care of business, and be gone before they knew what hit them. You don't want to advertise that kind of capability.

※

In 2014, Google mucky-muck Alan Eustace stepped into the record books with a parachute drop from 41,419 meters, reaching a falling velocity of 1,322 kph—that's Mach 1.1. If you are not impressed by that, you should be! Since there didn't seem to be any reason to better this, his record has stood the test of time.

The Teams had no reason to bring down the Eustace records; after all, that's not what we're about. But, we were nearly halfway there, and I would be lying if I told you we didn't talk about it. We were pretty sure, however, that Naval Special Warfare Group Five had no intention of spending its tight budget on an exotic balloon. So…I'm not sure why we didn't see it coming. Blame our narrow focus on the immediate job at hand. We let the senior officers handle the big picture.

EQUATORIAL PACIFIC—SLINGSHOT

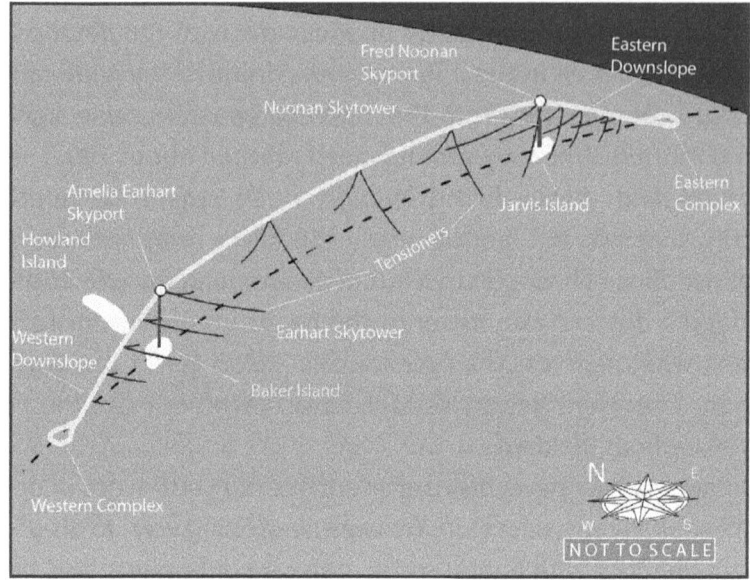

Figure 1—The Slingshot Space Launch Loop

I have to interrupt this tale to bring you up to speed on *Slingshot*. Yeah, I know, some of you already know all about the new Space Launch Loop stretching between Baker and Jarvis Islands in the equatorial Pacific. For the rest of you, try to visualize a five-centimeter-diameter soft-iron tube moving at nearly twelve kps, enclosed in a slightly larger stationary tube that starts a few meters below the ocean surface about 350 klicks west of Baker Island, rises to eighty klicks, and follows the curvature of the Earth for about 1,800 klicks to Jarvis Island, and then descends to a Complex east of Jarvis that is a mirror-image of the Complex to the west of Baker—and then it turns around and does the entire thing again in reverse. Now picture two elevator-like skytowers that connect each island to a skyport eighty klicks overhead. Stabilizing tensioners attached between the tube and ocean bottom maintain stability for the entire gossamer structure.

And here's the kicker. You get into a capsule on Baker Island, ride the skytower to the Amelia Earhart Skyport, attach magnetically to the rail (what they call the tube) just like an earthbound Maglev train, and several minutes later you are on your way to high Earth orbit, the Moon, or wherever, without the thundering rockets that we had to use until just a few years ago. Or…instead of launching into space, you can stay on the rail, slow yourself down with kick thrusters attached to your capsule, and debark at the Fred Noonan Skytower over Jarvis Island.

EQUATORIAL PACIFIC—HOWLAND ISLAND

And that's exactly what we did, Lt. Nelson, Senior Chief Boldt, and me and my six squadmates. Once again, I was the chosen jumper. No matter how you cut it, every time we did this, as the first choice, I racked up additional points, so that my stock-in-trade continued to grow over my squadmates. Not that they really minded. When it was all said and done, we were in it together, and they would get their turns—presuming I survived—with the benefit of my jump and the improvements I suggested. The goal this time, as you may have figured, was a *Gryphon* jump from 80,000 meters, with a 379-klick horizontal flight northeast to Kiritimati Island. The plan called for me to arrive on Kiritimati with twenty-five klicks of fuel left. Lt. Nelson and Senior Chief Boldt would monitor me by Link all the way, and we had comms available, although we did not really know how much back-and-forth we would have.

Anyway, we landed at Amelia Earhart International Airport on Howland Island, just a few klicks north of the Equator and Baker Island. The sky was filled with thousands of birds—mostly sooty terns, lesser frigatebirds, and masked boobies, I was told. The guys running the show had found a way to keep the birds away from incoming and outgoing aircraft, but otherwise, they were everywhere. It was pretty amazing. The folks here told me that the eco-terrorists who tried to bring down *Slingshot* somehow got the idea that it was an ecological hazard. From everything I could see, however, there are more birds now, more fish now, and we can get to space without dumping thousands of tons of pollutants into the air. The way I add it up, everybody wins.

EQUATORIAL PACIFIC—BAKER ISLAND

Our transit to Baker was just like so many other Chinook rides we had made over the past several years, except for the birds. They flew the distance with us and seemed to avoid the rotary wings instinctively. Once we landed, a bus took us to the Socket Complex, where we were briefed on the lightweight spacesuits we would wear. Launch Loop International (LLI) management wanted their own medical people to examine us—CYA, I guess. So, we were examined by this diver-EMT chick, Apryl Searson, who somehow managed to be both professional and beguiling simultaneously. I think everyone on my squad hit on her, but she reminded us that in a few minutes we would be some 2,000 klicks to the east, and she had better things to do than wait around for some horny sailors—even if they were SEALS. Nevertheless, when Apryl finished examining me, she stood on her tiptoes and whispered in my ear, "Good luck, Tiger!" followed by a fleeting kiss. Go figure! My heart rate must have hit 140, and the name stuck! The guys have been calling me *Tiger* ever since.

We donned our suits, carried our transparent globular helmets, and trudged toward the launch area. The capsule looked like a small, streamlined, light-rail car. Gull-wing doors that exposed the entire inside of the capsule opened on the left side. We slipped into memory-foam seats that accommodated us beautifully, and strapped in with over-the-shoulder harnesses that snapped in our laps. The nine of us, counting Lt. Nelson, fit into the capsule just fine, but the Socket Controller wouldn't let us take the wing with us, because of its hypergolic fuel load.

"Don't worry," he said. "It'll follow by five minutes in a freight capsule."

The trip up was exhilarating. Shortly after we tilted to vertical, I felt a faint tug that rapidly increased to about the same pressure produced by a chick sitting on my chest. I could just hear the high-pitched whine of the gyrostabilizer in the back. I heard an extended whoosh and turned my head to see fleecy clouds whip past the window. Seventeen seconds later (I counted them), and eight kilometers above the ground, the capsule shuddered. "Passing the sound barrier," a soft woman's voice floated through the capsule from concealed speakers. A few seconds later, the weight on my chest decreased slowly until I felt completely normal. Back to one gee. The capsule shuddered again, accompanied by a clank as the capsule shifted from the boost cable to the lift cable. The whooshing faded as the capsule, rising at more than 400 meters per second, left most of the Earth's air behind as it entered the rarified air of the upper stratosphere. There was no vibration, no sense of movement at all—it was if we were still on the ground. I looked out my port, but all I saw was an increasingly dark sky.

The sensation of being on the ground seemed to last forever, but it actually lasted for only three minutes. At seventy-two kilometers above the ground, the capsule released its hold on the lift cable and commenced its final eight-kilometer freefall to the skyport. My initial, completely unexpected, reaction was panic as all my weight disappeared. My body knew I was falling. Despite my intellect, every fiber in my being shouted *Falling… Falling!* To my embarrassment, my gorge rose in reaction. I swallowed hard to quell my stomach, and gripped my armrests fiercely as I fought to keep from hurling my stomach contents. After about a minute-and-a-half, I heard a clank as the capsule clamped to the frictionless motion deflector connecting the lift cable to the Amelia Earhart Skyport. I felt weight return, and my nausea completely disappeared as a gantry tilted us to horizontal.

To my amusement, I noticed that one of my guys actually did hurl—into a bag, fortunately.

Since the jump was to be from *Fred Noonan Skyport* over Jarvis Island, the plan called for us to transit right through *Amelia Earhart Skyport*, and ride the rail to *Noonan*. As our capsule glided into the capsule bay, the disembodied soft female voice we had heard earlier informed us that our seats would rotate 180 degrees for the reverse launch down the rail. Following that rotation, the gantry moved the capsule along the track with a slight jerk, and across to the rail. The capsule moved back against the kick thruster, where a clank signaled its successful attachment. Then the gantry gripping the capsule performed a half-turn, and the capsule shuddered slightly as the clamp attached a launch pouch. The disembodied voice commenced a short countdown.

"Five…four…three…two…one…zero…"

EQUATORIAL PACIFIC—FRED NOONAN SKYPORT (JARVIS ISLAND)

I felt myself pushed back into my seat with a very tolerable amount of g-force. It felt much like stepping hard on the accelerator of a car, and keeping it there for a while—eleven minutes, to be exact. Then a soft chime signaled the seat rotation just before the thruster ignited. I began to feel a bit uneasy with the realization that we were careening toward the skyport at several klicks per second, but the feeling vanished with the sound of the thruster. Almost immediately, I began to feel the deceleration as I was pushed back into my seat again. As before, the feeling was not uncomfortable. Before I had a chance to think much about the process, the deceleration lifted as the capsule glided into the bay at *Fred Noonan Skyport*. Several clanks signaled removal of spent thruster and the launch pouch, and then the gantry moved the capsule to the bay where hydraulic rams created a seal with the lock, and the gull-wing doors lifted.

We disembarked into the skyport, where we were welcomed by the six-person duty shift. Their job was to deal with people and cargo, manhandle incoming and outgoing kick thrusters, and generally ensure that *Noonan Skyport* ran as designed. We spent a few minutes admiring the view from eighty klicks in the sky through the large polymer windows. I gotta tell you, it's damned impressive, any way you slice it. The horizon was out a thousand-ten klicks of empty ocean in every direction, except for two islands, Kiritimati—my destination—at 379 klicks on a northeasterly bearing, and Tabuaeran Atoll at 475 klicks slightly right of north. I thought I could see a smudge where Kiritimati should have been, but Tabuaeran was half-way to the horizon and invisible to the naked eye. The ocean was deep blue, covered by streaks of brilliant white cloud swirls in opposing patterns to the north and south. Oh yeah, there was one more island eighty klicks directly below us. The lower deck of the skyport boasted a large window that looked directly down on Jarvis. The Jarvis Skytower met the skyport right beside this window and rapidly disappeared toward the island below.

From both decks, the fragile-appearing rail simply faded from view toward the west. And the sky above—oh my! The sky above was a deep black punctuated with more stars than I had ever seen. The Milky Way stretched from horizon to horizon, a brilliant band of countless multi-colored points of light. I had never experienced anything like it! I could have spent all day admiring the view.

True to the Socket Controller's word, a few minutes after we disembarked, the cargo capsule arrived carrying my *Gryphon-7*. Since we were there to do a job, Lt. Nelson pushed a bit, and we reluctantly stopped playing tourists, donned our helmets, checked comms, and—under the watchful eye of a female shift member—passed through the lock into the evacuated capsule arrival bay. The Lieutenant remained in the passenger area to brief the crew on what we were doing, and to keep control of what little security about the operation remained. Normally, hydraulic rams press a capsule to the lock seal so the gull-wing doors can open into the skyport. The cargo capsule, however, remained inside the bay so we could access the wing directly.

You have to remember that we were not there for publicity, for the most part anyway. We needed to test the limits of *Gryphon-7*. This was an entirely new kind of weapon, or perhaps *delivery system* is a better way to characterize it. It was imperative that we test its limits. We had to know its operational boundaries. That's why we were there. So, we pulled the rolled-up *Gryphon-7* from the cargo capsule and laid it out for setup. Once the carapace had inflated, and the systems checked, two of the guys held it upright while I securely fastened the wide Velcro band across my middle. This was particularly important because I would be hanging from these straps for the entire flight. I slipped my arms and legs through the retaining straps, and the guys tightened them. I could have done this myself, but it was much easier with help. I wrapped my hands around the grip controllers—I was ready.

Basically, the skyport capsule bay is an elongated cylinder with atmospheric seals at both ends. When we passed through the lock from the one-atmosphere skyport main deck, we entered what was virtually the vacuum of space. Lt. Nelson joined us after I was winged up, and we were ready. He gave me a quick once-over—not that I needed it, but if something happened to me, it was his ass. Besides, I think he really cared for me and the rest of the guys. We walked along the rail through the open seal at the other end of the cylinder, the one the capsules pass through to catch the rail. Overhead, the capsule gantry waited silently for the next arriving capsule, that was probably sitting in the launch bay on Baker waiting for us to get the hell out of the way. We stepped onto a catwalk that looked like expanded metal but was actually a special polymer that hardened under UV light to a strength many times greater than steel with a tiny fraction of its weight. In front of us, the rail in its casing looked unbelievably fragile. It seemed to hang in mid-air, I mean mid-space, suspended inside a twenty-meter-long one-and-a-half-meter-wide half-cylinder that extended several meters out from the skyport. It was constructed from the same light-weight material as the catwalk. We all attached safety lines from our suits to several anchor points on the catwalk, and then gingerly walked along the grate at the bottom of the horizontal half-cylinder.

It was an incredibly eerie feeling, knowing that there was nothing beneath me but eighty klicks of empty—well, I guess that at least half of that was air, technically, but it sure looked like empty, except for some fleecy clouds passing below. As you probably can guess, heights don't really bother me, so I had no problem standing right at the edge of the grate. Besides, I was still attached to my safety line.

I made sure of my orientation. The smudge that was Kiritimati Island lay 379 klicks over my right shoulder—and eighty down. One final Link check, and high-fives all around, although that's hard to do in a spacesuit with a *Gryphon-7* on my back, and I launched.

EQUATORIAL PACIFIC—GRYPHON FLIGHT

Immediately, I was in familiar territory, no different really from my 15,000-meter jump. I tumbled straight down, because there was no air to support me. No nausea, though; even my innards knew what was happening

*Figure 2—Howland, Baker, Jarvis & Kiribati Islands
– Flight of the Gryphon*

as I broke the tumble and staged myself horizontally. First, I extended my tail. "Tail extended and locked," I reported. My *Gryphon* was now two meters long. Next, I spread my wings to their full three-meter-wingspan. "Wings extended and locked," I reported, drily. "Rocket ignited, heading vector set to zero-four-niner-decimal-five-four, horizontal velocity two-hundred kph," I reported as I ignited my rocket, got myself pointed in the right direction, and gunned it until I reached my designated horizontal velocity.

With my house-keeping tasks out of the way, I relaxed against my straps, settled into my belly-band, and located my goal in the heads-up. I was dead on. I flattened myself as near to horizontal as possible, and then checked my drop rate. I caught my breath, and I imagine that my readouts in *Noonan* displayed a jump in heart-rate. I was plummeting downward at nearly Mach 1 and still accelerating—after only thirty seconds of freefall.

"Are you guys getting this?" I asked with a level of excitement that even I could hear.

"Piece of cake, Tiger," the Lieutenant drawled.

"Nothin' you ain't done before," the Senior Chief added. "Keep the chatter comin'!"

"I'm pushing Mach two, guys." I was passing sixty seconds. "No drag that I can feel."

Thirty seconds later, the Senior Chief said, "Your suit temp is way high. Can you feel it?"

"You're kiddin', right? I'm doing Mach two-point-four, ferchrissake… whaddya expect?" He was right, though, it was more than a little warm, but I was beginning to bite some air. I had fallen 40,000 meters and covered only five horizontal klicks thus far. Fortunately, my forward velocity was increasing as I grabbed more air.

I was tempted to kick in the rocket again, but the Lieutenant must have read my mind. "Conserve your fuel, Tiger," he told me. "We got your back."

I agreed, I guess. I had about twenty-five klicks of fuel left, and I really needed to save it for Kiritimati. Remember, I could push myself for thirty klicks on rocket alone, but I had no idea what I might find at my goal, so he was right, I needed to conserve fuel. That meant no climbing under any circumstances, and no level flight either, if I wanted to have fuel when I got there. The increasing air resistance let me convert some of my downward velocity to lift. That, plus air drag actually slowed my fall to about half, so that as I passed 30,000 meters about thirty-six seconds later, I was falling at only about Mach 0.8.

You gotta see this in context. I was falling from 80,000 meters, just me and my *Gryphon*. If I did nothing, I would be a cooked piece of dead meat by the time I hit the water, but I had already done something. My fall speed was less than half of what it had been, and my forward velocity had increased to just short of 600 kph. This got me another six horizontal klicks and an *attaboy* from the Senior Chief. I was pretty busy right about then and had little time for conversation, but I grunted my appreciation. I still had a glide ratio of only one-to-two—one forward for every two down, which sucks, but I was gaining on it.

At this height, I had a pretty good air bite, so that seventy-two seconds later, I was falling through 20,000 meters at 500 kph with a glide ratio of about two-to-one, meaning my forward velocity was just about Mach 1.0. I had chewed up another twenty-four horizontal klicks. This is where I really started to grab air. I retained most of my forward velocity but dropped my descent to only fifty.

Twelve minutes later, I passed through 10,000 meters and had traveled a full 220 klicks closer to Kiritimati. That left 124 to go with 10,000 meters of air under me. My forward speed was now a relatively slow 250 with a full ten-to-one rate of descent of 20. That would get me 125 klicks, which left me a bonus klick plus another twenty-five under power. Things were looking pretty good right about then.

That's when Lt. Nelson commented wryly, "I concur with your numbers."

"So…I been talkin' in my sleep again," I said, and got a chuckle from the Senior Chief.

"Looks like we're picking up some weather ahead," the Lieutenant added. "Off to your right a bit."

I was cruising straight and true, and was passing through 5,000 meters with about seventy-five klicks left to fly, when I spotted it off to the right and ahead at about twenty degrees. It was what they call a tropical squall down on the water. These guys appear and disappear almost randomly. None of us saw this one coming. From where I was, however, a wall of cloud, cumulonimbus calvus actually, seemed to rise right out of the ocean to the east of Kiritimati to a height of about 3,000 meters. "Are you guys getting this?" I asked. Someone acknowledged—I'm not sure who.

As I moved forward, the squall's relative bearing to me did not change. "It looks like that sucker and I are going to collide right over Kiritimati," I said.

"Looks that way," the Lieutenant agreed.

"You can always ditch," the Senior Chief quipped, "if you think it's more than you can handle."

Even though his comments were half-jest, he was right. This was turning out not to be your normal squall, but rather the mother of all rapidly moving thunderstorms. I really did not want to be anywhere near that sonofabitch. But that storm and I had an unavoidable meeting with destiny.

Worst case scenario, I thought to myself, *is that I got a kiss from Apryl before Mother Nature kicks my butt.*

"You have all the luck!" the Senior Chief said with a chuckle.

"Well, shit! Thinkin' out loud again," I said back. "Gotta stop doing that."

※

Kiritimati is an elongated atoll about seventy-five klicks long and thirty at its widest, at an angle of about forty-five degrees west of north. From my aerial perspective, it occupied a swath of about forty klicks, which meant that when the storm and I rendezvoused over the island, I had no place to go. I suppose I could have ditched before the storm hit, as the Senior Chief had coyly suggested, but that seemed like a cop-out.

"I'm wearing a spacesuit, guys," I said. "So long as I don't crash, I should be okay."

"We're considering your options," Lt. Nelson said.

With just a few minutes left, and already feeling the effects of the storm, I decided to put my equipment to a full-bore test, no matter what the bosses said. After all, I was wearing a full spacesuit strapped to a *Gryphon-7*, and I was here—they were up there. "Screw it!" I said. "I'm doin' it!"

I pointed my rig at the storm's heart, powered the rocket for a few seconds, and plunged into the wall of cloud. Instantly, I lost all visual orientation, except the visual sensation that I was moving really fast through something.

"Talk to me!" Lt. Nelson said.

"Woo-oo," I answered as my twenty kph fall rate instantly changed to fifty kph rising, and my belly-band pressed hard against my midriff. I was accelerating upward rapidly. "You guys still with me?" I shouted, as the squall raged around me, soaking everything.

"We got you, Tiger!" That was Senior Chief Boldt.

A hundred seconds later, I was flung out of the top of the thunderhead, fully 3,000 meters over Kiritimati, and rising at 100 kph. The wet had turned to a layer of ice that began flaking off as I continued to rise. Below me, lightning played furiously between the thunderheads. "I still have twenty-five klicks of fuel, and now I got thirty of glide," I said, as I wrestled back full control of the *Gryphon* and cleared the top of the thunderhead that had vomited me into the sky. "Oops!" I hadn't intended to say that aloud. "I'm falling back in," I said as I found myself plunging headfirst back down into the lightning-filled inferno, trailing ice shards behind me.

"Trust your instruments," the Lieutenant said quietly to help me regain control.

I used a burst of fuel to force myself into a horizontal attitude, and oriented the *Gryphon* with the heads-up GPS. I was doing 250 and rising again. This time I exited the cloud top with more grace, heading northeast away from Kiritimati at 200 kph. Once again, I was covered with ice, and once again, I had a full thirty klicks of glide available. "I'm gonna swing a wide arc to the north and come in under the trailing edge of the storm," I commented. "I'll land nice-as-you-please at the edge of their airport runway." I was only about twenty klicks to the northeast at about 3,000 meters, so I had plenty of air. At least, that's how I had it figured.

"Where the fuck did that come from?" I didn't even see the airstream that captured me. One moment I was flying free and clear, looking for a good place to land, and the next, I was slammed into the north wall of the squall, but this time, instead of rising, I was falling—fast. Things were happening very quickly, and I had no choice but to fire the rocket to stop my descent and gain some horizontal traction. The squall was petering out behind me as it passed Kiritimati, but I was fighting like hell to keep from crashing into the waves directly below. By the time I was back in control, Kiritimati was several klicks behind me to the east, and ahead of me lay over 3,000 klicks of open ocean. "You guys still with me?" I panted, breathless from the heavy exertion. I whipped around, fired the rocket to maintain a five-meter-altitude, and took aim for the center of the island several klicks ahead of me.

"Yeah…nice save!" Senior Chief Boldt's voice was unemotional and calming.

KIRITIMATI ISLAND

My fuel gauge indicated five klicks of fuel remaining, but I had no reference for gauging the distance of a thirteen-meter-high atoll from five meters over the waves. Ahead of me, I could see the open arms of the atoll embracing the inner lagoon, the tiny hamlet of London to the north,

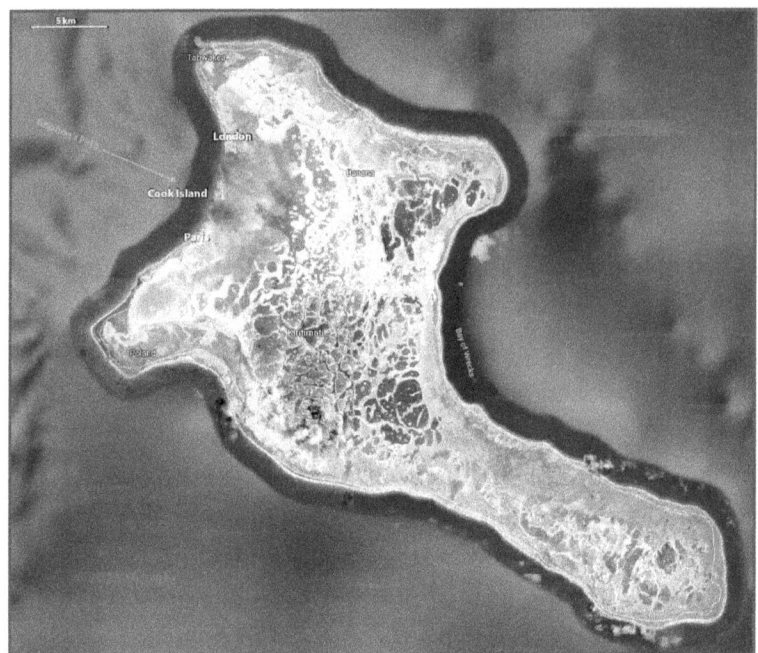

Figure 3—Kiritimati Island –Gryphon splashdown

and even smaller Paris about three klicks to the south. Directly between them lay uninhabited Cook Island—my immediate goal, I decided. And it could have been one or ten klicks away—I simply didn't know.

"Can I make Cook?" I asked.

"There's a chance," the Lieutenant said.

"By my reckoning," the Senior Chief added, "you're still three klicks out, but you only got two-and-a-half klicks of fuel." He paused. "Try flappin' your arms…"

The water beneath me shallowed noticeably as the wave tops grew higher. One-and-a-half minutes later, with me still beyond the breaker line about 200 meters from shore, the rocket coughed and quit. I hit the drink, unceremoniously, belly first.

"You okay, Tiger?" Senior Chief Boldt asked.

"Fine," I said, "working my way ashore." The *Gryphon-7* was the best wingsuit I had ever flown, but it sucked as a surfboard, especially when I was face-down, strapped to the bottom. I retracted the tail and wings, unstrapped my hands and legs, and commenced an ungainly dogpaddle. It took a while, but I was finally just beyond the breaker line. I loosened the Velcro belly-band and pulled myself loose from the *Gryphon*. I grabbed it by the tail, pulled it underwater, and flipped it end-for-end.

"What's goin' on?" It was the Senior Chief.

"Goin' surfin'," I said. I pulled myself on top of the inverted *Gryphon*, knelt near the nose, and waited for the next big wave. I had to wait only about thirty seconds, and then I started paddling for all I was worth. The wave picked me up, and I started moving down its face. I jumped to my feet, set myself to a proper surfing stance, and pressed down with my back foot, so the *Gryphon's* stabilizers took a bite. I turned left pretty-as-you-please, and glided at an angle down the eight-meter-high wave face…that is, for all of about two seconds, followed by a spectacular wipeout and a perfect over-the-falls tumble as the wave whipped both me and the *Gryphon* down to the sandy bottom, and then back up through the churning water column so we emerged behind the wave.

"You okay, Tiger?" The Senior Chief actually sounded concerned.

"Yeah—I'll tell you about it after. Pretty busy right now." I was watching the next wave and trying to get stomach-down flat on the upside-down *Gryphon* before it reached me.

This time I stayed flat, moving my hands just enough to get a bit of an angle on the wave face so I wouldn't plow into the bottom with the wave crest crashing over me. It wasn't very elegant, but I didn't wipeout. The *Gryphon* finally settled to the wet white sand as the wave receded. I wasted no time in grabbing the *Gryphon* and hurrying up the beach to where the sand was definitely dry.

"Status report!" It was Lt. Nelson. I briefed him on the final wet fifteen minutes of my flight and made some suggestions for dealing with future water entries. They were mostly about stability in the water and a means of powered propulsion. It was only a few minutes later that a Zodiac with four SEALS from the second squad arrived on the lagoon side of Cook Island.

DAEDALUS—FINALE

I'm sure you know the rest of the story, so I won't repeat it here. I survived, and then I survived my fifteen minutes of fame. My *Gryphon-7* hangs in the Smithsonian, but you know that, too.

The Jarvis drop has been accomplished probably a hundred times since then, but mine was the one with all the excitement. We've moved on to bigger and better things now, and have our sights set on a drop from low-earth-orbit. I'll let you know when it finally happens.

DAEDALUS LEO
SWIC Drop from Low Earth Orbit

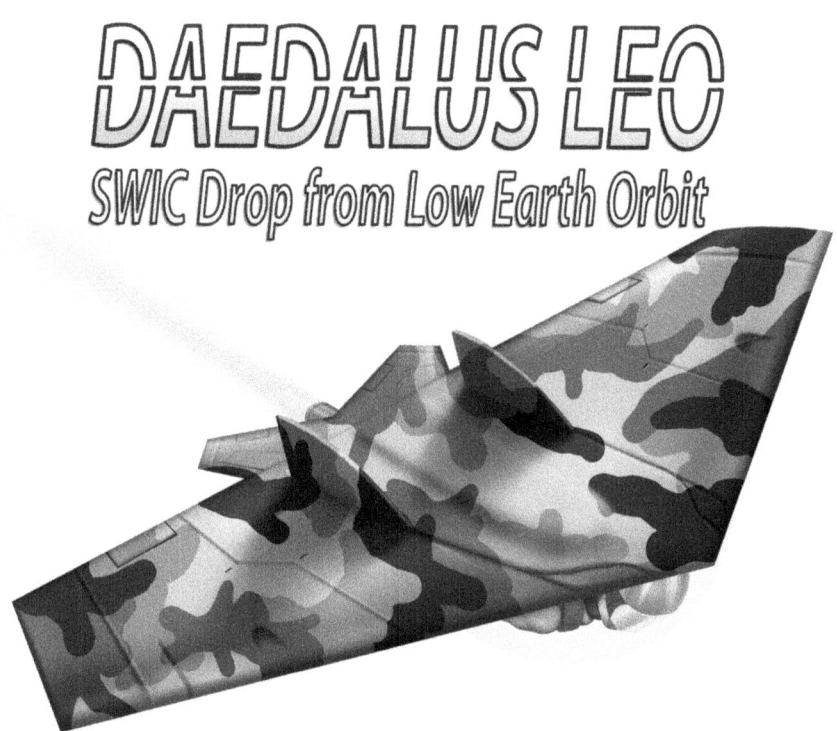

Chapter Two

CHAPTER TWO

DAEDALUS LEO

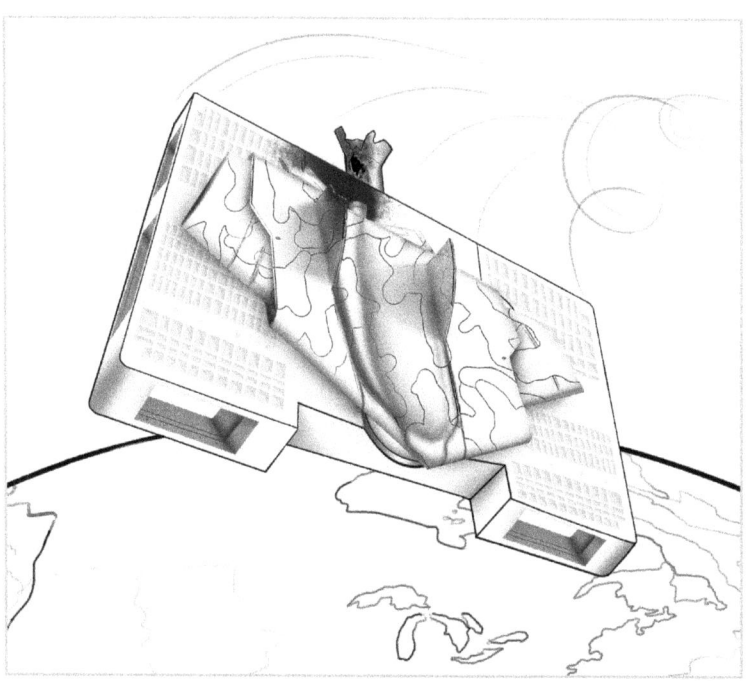

Figure 4—Gryphon and pallet with Tiger Baily in LEO in an uncontrolled tumble.

LOW EARTH ORBIT

"What the fuck!" I yelped as the rear of my *Gryphon-10* pallet tilted sharply upward while the nose yawed to the right. Then the whole thing started to tumble in a spiral fashion as the kick thruster continued its burn. Mother wasn't stopping it, so I activated the manual jettison override. I watched the burning kick thruster spiral ahead of me and then flare out. I lost it in the glare of the morning sun.

"I got a problem here, Control," I said as calmly as I could manage. I described what had happened from my limited perspective. "Mother, deploy the tethered holocam and make a full external inspection," I ordered as I began to get my act together.

"Tiger, we are calculating your modified orbital parameters right now," Master Chief Boldt told me with his calming voice. "Okay…here it is. You are nominally still at one-hundred-sixty klicks, but your orbit has shifted right by twenty-two-point-five-degrees. That passes over central Mexico, well south of Baja. You're stable, but you have to get control of your tumble so we can calculate a new set of drop parameters."

"Roger," I said.

"Tethered holocam deployed," Mother said softly.

Mother controlled the bird-size tethered holocam to ensure that it maintained a stable position relative to my corkscrew. Using additional short gas bursts, I maneuvered the holocam down the length of the pallet and *Gryphon-10*, looking for damage.

"Jesus H…," I muttered as it moved to my stern. "Are you getting this, Control?"

"Roger, we are."

The back end of the pallet was partially melted, and a large chunk was missing from my right fin.

"Mother, can I survive reentry with that fin damage?"

"Negative, Tiger," Mother said softly, "Probability of complete structure failure one hundred percent."

CORONADO—SAN DIEGO—SEVERAL DAYS EARLIER

Derek "Tiger" Baily—you may remember me. The *Gryphon-7*? My 80,000-meter base jump from the Fred Noonan Skyport on *Slingshot*? Well…so much for fifteen minutes of fame, but you still can see *Gryphon-7* at the Smithsonian, and you can read about my exploit if you dig a little bit.

I'm still with the Teams—the U.S. Navy SEALS, but now I command SEALS Winged Insertion Command Three, SWIC-3 for short. I suspect somebody in the hierarchy goofed after I completed that 80,000-meter base jump, but I got orders to OCS—that's Officer Candidate School for you non-military types—and ended up back at SWIC-3 as a freshly minted Butter Bar—Ensign. We continued our *Gryphon* development with me as XO under Lt.Cdr. Tom Spitzer. Senior Chief Jerry Boldt was still with us, in line for Master Chief. By the time my old CO Brad Nelson made Captain, they gave him command of SWIC, assigned Tom as his XO, and I got command of SWIC-3 along with early promotion to Lt.Cdr. Like I said, somebody really goofed up there, but who am I to argue with them? Besides, they sent me Lt. Jim Fox as XO. He had come up through the SEAL ranks like me, and I couldn't have gotten a better man to back me up.

My assignment, SWIC-3's assignment, was probably impossible to accomplish. I figured that just made it interesting. All Capt. Nelson wanted was for SWIC-3 to do a *Gryphon* drop from LEO—Low Earth Orbit.

CORONADO—GRYPHON-10

Gryphon-7 had been relegated to the annals of SEAL history. *Gryphon-8* incorporated the structural changes resulting from my water landing, causing the craft to act more like a surfboard when upside down in the water, and giving it external propulsion—basically incorporating a waterjet. *Gryphon-9* changed a lot of things. It had larger wings with more fuel capacity, more powerful jet with throttle control, longer tail, and more intuitive control interface.

Gryphon-10 is the baby we would use for the LEO drop. It had some radical changes, including full body armor with circulating fuel for heat protection, an increased surface area using dimples, wrinkles, and rolls that dramatically boosted heat shedding, and it incorporated a new type of polymer that was stronger, lighter, and more heat resistant than anything before. The biggest change, however, was the guidance computer unit—we called it Mother—that was designed to act on its calculations before the human pilot was even aware of them. *Gryphon-10* was still man-transportable, although more ungainly than the old *Gryphon-7* model. Its unpowered glide ratio was 14-1, and it could fly 100 level klicks under power.

Unlike *Gryphon-7* that started at eighty klicks with zero velocity, *Gryphon-10* would start at 160 klicks moving at orbital velocity. To survive the jump, *Gryphon-10* had to shed as much velocity as possible as quickly as possible. We needed to get from Mach 26 down to about Mach 3. What we'd do was to dip down into the atmosphere shedding speed until drag brought the temperature to the limit, and then skip back out of the atmosphere to let the suit cool off. Then back in again, shed more speed, heat to the limit, and back out to cool off. And again…and again…using a bit of fuel for each dip until we slowed to about Mach 3. Then dip for the last time, and stretch out the glide for max distance—and land at the desired destination. We ran the problem in reverse, letting the computers work out the number and details of the skips to specify where in our equatorial orbit we would need to commence the drop. We threw every variable we could think of at the problem and calculated the drop for 10,000 different scenarios.

CORONADO—MAX

To help plan the drop, we constructed Max—a full-scale simulator that cost a good deal more than the actual *Gryphon-10*. Everyone in SWIC-3 ran Max dozens of times. I did the first run and crashed and burned big time. With practice, we got the system down and a feel for what to do during each skip into the atmosphere.

Now, here's the rub. Everything we did up to this point was theoretical—even with Max. We gave Max every scrap of reentry information we could find, everything we knew about upper atmosphere weather, every bit of physics that could possibly bear on the problem. Mother knew everything Max knew and was connected to worldwide live feeds. In a real drop, Mother would know everything possible about the path ahead, and everything Max had done in similar situations during simulation runs. Mother would have every possible edge to give us the desired outcome. Yet…until we actually made the first drop, all we had were numbers that we hoped made sense.

SLINGSHOT—EQUATORIAL PACIFIC

Beyond Max, we ran real jumps using the full *Gryphon-10* from Fred Noonan Skyport on Slingshot to Kiritimati and even to Tabuaeran Atoll about 100 klicks further north. We didn't challenge a squall like I had done on the first Kiritimati jump, but I was confident that the *Gryphon-10* could have handled it with ease. We did soft belly landings, near-shore water landings, and blue-water landings. We had no problems—none at all.

That was encouraging, to say the least.

LEO—UNMANNED DROP

I sent Master Chief Boldt to Baker Island with four SWIC-3 members. They lifted to Amelia Earhart Skyport with the empty *Gryphon-10* attached to a cargo pallet. After ensuring that everything was fully ready for the drop, they launched the pallet with its load.

The process of obtaining a circular orbit was automatic until the actual launch of *Griffon-10*. I controlled that from our Flight Control Center (FCC) at Coronado.

※

I initiated the drop sequence and then sat at the Command Console, watching Mother do her thing. We shed velocity with three dips, and a few minutes later, *Gryphon-10* was circling about two klicks above San Diego Bay, shedding the last of her forward velocity and altitude.

Ten minutes later, everyone but me pushed through the FCC door as *Gryphon-10* spiraled to a picture-perfect landing ten meters from the door.

CORONADO—MANNED DROP PREP

Every SWIC-3 member wanted to do the first manned LEO drop—including me. They chose me to do the first static drop from Slingshot back in my enlisted days because I was easily the most experienced wingsuit man in the Teams—that's why they recruited me in the first place. But now, I was part of *they*. I still was the most experienced wingsuit man in the Teams, more so now than ever. Furthermore, I had more experience in *Gryphon-10*, both in Max and for real in drops, than anyone else—close to as much as everyone else combined. Not only did I have more Max drops under my belt, but I also had more Max disasters, and I had found creative ways to extricate myself from several of them. But I also was CO of SWIC-3. Despite what you see in holobroadcasts, commanding officers do not normally do everything personally. They surround themselves with good people, and then they assign the best people to the task at hand.

I know that Capt. Nelson had several high-level discussions with his Team boss, and I suspect the discussions went even higher. What we were attempting was still classified above Top Secret, but our success would give a dramatic new insertion capability to the generals and admirals who make the big plans. I'm sure the interest went all the way to the White House.

In the end, I was ordered to the assignment, Lt. Jim Fox was given temporary command of SWIC-3, and Master Chief Jerry Boldt was temporarily assigned as Executive Officer. Senior Chief Bob Baxter took over for Master Chief Boldt, and the Team members supplied their best efforts in support.

HOWLAND & BAKER ISLANDS—PRELAUNCH

As I departed Coronado for North Island Airfield with Senior Chief Baxter and six SWIC-3 Team members, I quipped to the rest of the Team, "This is the first leg of my roundtrip, guys. I'll see you back here in two-and-a-half days." It turned out that was not exactly how it happened, but we didn't know that then.

We had already spent three days going over every single part of *Gryphon-10* and its launch pallet, and we did the same with its twin, a fully operational backup system. Then I went over both systems again myself—just to be sure. Both systems waited for us strapped down in a big Navy supersonic transport aircraft on the North Island tarmac under a brilliant blue sky speckled with puffy cirrocumulus clouds.

The entire remaining SWIC-3 team and Capt. Nelson himself saw us off. We jetted down the runway, lifted through the sparse clouds into the stratosphere, and turned toward Hawaii as we accelerated to nearly Mach 2.

Four hours later, with one refueling stop in Hawaii, we rolled to a stop at Amelia Earhart International Airport under a blistering equatorial sun. Thousands of sooty terns, lesser frigatebirds, and masked boobies filled the sky, kept clear of aircraft by a sonic system that was inaudible to the human ear.

At the end of the tarmac near the entrance to Launch Loop International (LLI) Howland headquarters, two Chinooks waited with cargo bays open, twin rotors drooping as if wilting in the hot tropical sun. Senior Chief Baxter and his six guys remained with the aircraft to supervise the unloading of the two pallets and their loading into the much tighter Chinook interiors.

I strolled slowly through the humid air toward the headquarters building to meet with the current Slingshot director, Sam Davidson. As I turned toward the double front doors, they opened and out walked Apryl Searson.

"Tiger Baily, as I live and breathe! It's really you, isn't it?" She ran up, threw her arms around my neck, and gave me a kiss the like of which I had not received in a very long time.

"I've been here several times in the last few months," I said. "Where were you?"

"Been at the Atlantic site working with Margo on the new launch loop," she said, nuzzling my neck. "What're you doing here?"

"If I told you, Apryl, I'd have to kill you," I said with a grin.

"Will you have any time for me before you leave for LEO?" she asked with a twinkle in her blue eyes.

"Schedule's pretty tight," I told her, "but a guy's gotta sleep…"

She stuck out her tongue at me. "…or not," she whispered as she disentangled herself. "When are you lifting to the skyport?"

"Later this afternoon, when we have thoroughly checked both systems out—both the Senior Chief and me."

"In these or your flightsuit?" she asked, stroking my chest.

"I'll change into my flightsuit after I talk with Sam," I told her.

※

I spent fifteen minutes with Sam Davidson. He had been briefed on our operation and was concerned about any possible hitch in his 24/7 schedule of throwing people and cargo into space. His launch operation was tight by any definition: One personnel or cargo capsule every three minutes, each adding to LLI's bottom line. That's 480 daily launches, typically broken down into 2,000 metric tons of cargo and eighty personnel capsules. That's a lot of freight and people, and my operation would impact it negatively.

"Sam," I said as I stood to leave, "I know we're cutting into your schedule, but you're being well paid for the inconvenience." I shook his hand. "Besides, think of the glory!"

He grinned and slapped my back as I left. "Good luck, Tiger! I'm glad it's you and not me."

※

Apryl was waiting for me outside Sam's door, my folded flightsuit in her arms. She winked and indicated with a toss of her blond, pixie-cut hair for me to follow her. Intrigued, I did, despite my tight schedule. We entered a small conference room. Apryl locked the door behind us, threw her arms around my neck, and wrapped her legs around my waist. She planted a kiss on me that eclipsed her earlier one on the steps.

After we came up for air, things progressed rapidly, and all I can say is that it was a good thing the room was soundproofed.

I left the conference room several minutes later, somewhat the worse for wear, dressed in my flightsuit—still pretty much on schedule. Apryl promised to give my clothing to Senior Chief Baxter.

※

By the time I got to the Chinooks, Senior Chief Baxter and his guys had both pallets loaded and were tightening straps over the fairings, cinching them to tie-downs in the chopper decks. Baxter split the guys up, and then he took one Chinook, and I took the other for the short flight to Baker Island.

The choppers landed right next to the loading rail and disgorged the pallets. An articulating boom crane loader rolled up under control of one of the socket crew who deftly hoisted the first pallet over the rail where another crew member attached it to a launch dolly directly behind the personnel capsule designated for us. Then he did the second one, that would remain at the socket, ready to lift should it be needed. Senior Chief Baxter carefully checked each component of each pallet-dolly unit, and then I did it again. Everything checked out.

Senior Chief Baxter glanced at me, and I nodded. "Board up!" he told the guys.

The five-minute trip up to Amelia Earhart Skyport was just as much of a rush as the first time.

AMELIA EARHART SKYPORT—PRELAUNCH

At Amelia Earhart Skyport, eighty klicks above Baker Island, the capsule tilted to horizontal, sealed against the skyport lock, and the door opened inward. There was Apryl Searson tossing me a coquettish smile. Apparently, she had caught the first available capsule following our tryst. As I stepped into the reception area, Apryl brushed my lips with hers and whispered in my ear, "Before you leave, Tiger, find three minutes for me!" Senior Chief Baxter pretended not to notice, but his guys all grinned at me. One flashed me a thumbs-up.

The capsule closed behind us, the lock sealed, and a gantry crane moved the capsule out of the way.

"Okay, guys, suit up!" Baxter ordered, and a minute or so later, the pallet arrived.

With skytower traffic stopped, the guys hustled through the personnel lock. They removed the fairing and stowed it, and then they prepped the pallet with its *Gryphon-10* payload, swinging the wingsuit pod cover to vertical on its hinges like a clamshell. Baxter once more examined every part of the pallet and wingsuit. If it was humanly possible, he was not going to let something happen to the Skipper (me!) on his watch during this historic LEO drop. He took his time, oblivious to the queued-up freight pallets and passenger capsules waiting down at Baker Socket. As he finished, he signaled to me in the main skyport lounge area to suit up for *my* final system check.

"Time to go," I said to Apryl, who was snuggled against me on a couch overlooking the broad, colorful band of stars that we know as the Milky Way; only out here, it looked more like a multi-colored, diamond-studded bracelet spanning the sky.

The skyport crew had left us alone during the setup and systems check, and even now, they gave us as much privacy as possible. Apryl nuzzled my neck and then kissed me passionately.

"Come back to me, Tiger, and tell me all about your fantastic adventure!"

Little did she or I know what lay in store.

✺

After disentangling myself from Apryl, I suited up. Our suits were an advanced version of the old NASA flightsuits incorporating high-pressure oxygen bottles and electronic carbon-dioxide scrubbers. A pair of TBH (Thomas, Bird, and Hellbaum) hypergolic jet boots that slipped over the suit feet and calves completed the getup. The boot fuel valves were controlled by a microswitch under each big toe.

I stepped through the personnel lock onto the dock and commenced a detailed inspection of the pallet and wingsuit. Like Senior Chief Baxter, I

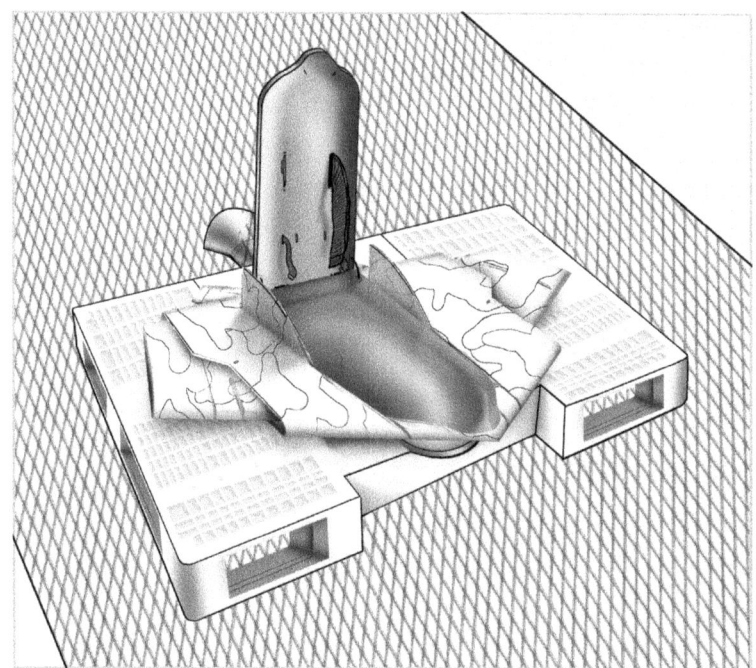

Figure 5—Gryphon and pallet on the Fred NoonanSkyport platform ready to receive a rider.

took my time. It was my ass on the line, and I wanted to be sure that everything was nominal.

My team stood around chatting quietly on their private circuit, watching everything I did to ensure I missed nothing. I kept open a private circuit with the Senior Chief and went through the checklist with him, item-by-item. I was focused for about a half-hour, and as I finished, I looked up at the transparent port between the dock and the skyport lounge. Apryl's face filled the port. I waved a gauntleted hand at her, and she blew a kiss back. My guys roared their approval, although I could only see this by the expressions on their faces—the dock remained silent.

I stepped onto the pallet, backed up against the pod cover, and allowed the crew to strap me in. Unlike *Gryphon-7*, where my arms were securely strapped to the wings, on the *Gryphon-10* my arms were free to move from the wings to my body within the encasing carapace. This was a lot more comfortable than the older version, but I still could not scratch my back. My legs were strapped in very much like the *Gryphon-7*, as was my body. Then the crew swung down the pod cover with me attached just like a closing clamshell. They sealed the edges all around, pressurized it, and checked for leaks.

So far, this was exactly like the several static drops I had already made from Fred Noonan Skyport in the *Gryphon-10*. As I felt the cool breeze from my air supply against my right cheek, I told the Senior Chief that I was ready for the final countdown.

AMELIA EARHART SKYPORT—LAUNCH

"Base, Bird—comm check."

"Loud and clear, Tiger." It was Master Chief Boldt. His calm voice was reassuring.

"We completed all checks and are transiting to the rail," I said. "Systems nominal up here."

"Roger that…Base systems nominal."

"Mother, state your status," Boldt ordered.

"Standing by to launch." Mother's voice did not sound artificial but rather had a soothing, contralto tone.

"We're ready when you are," Boldt said.

I felt the gantry lift the pallet and move down the track. I knew the routine, but my direct vision was limited to down and a bit side to side. I could turn my head inside the transparent helmet, but the helmet was locked into the carapace. I activated my heads-up display so I could monitor what was going on around me. The gantry moved the pallet to the kick thruster platform, and then backward to attach the kick thruster. The kick thruster is a reigniteable solid-fuel rocket. This always worried me a bit. I'm not a rocket scientist, but I know a lot about rockets. Shutting down a burning solid-fuel rocket is no simple task. LLI did this using an iris-like, very strong magnetic field to slice through the solid fuel column just above the burn. They had never experienced a misfire, so the odds were in my favor, but this time *I* was riding the pallet. I wasn't safely tucked into a capsule that could withstand atmospheric reentry in case something went wrong.

The gantry moved the pallet over the rail, where a launch pouch was attached. Its purpose was to couple magnetically to the rail, accelerating the pallet at three-gees until it reached LEO orbital velocity. Simple to tell, but complex in doing.

"Final systems check," I announced over the general circuit. "Bird systems nominal."

"Mother nominal." Mother's calming voice filled my helmet.

"Flight Control nominal," Master Chief Boldt said. "On my count: Five, four, three, two, one…Launch!"

SLINGSHOT RAIL—COUPLED

One moment we—the pallet, *Gryphon-10*, and I—were hovering above the rail. The next, we surged forward, gently at first, and then rapidly built to three-gees, with me taking the gees through my body to my feet. I could still feel the Velcro straps securing my legs inside the upper carapace. I knew my legs were surrounded by the carapace and could not collapse, but the feel of the straps was reassuring anyway.

Exactly four minutes after launch, Mother rotated the pallet 45° to the left. Twenty-seven seconds later and 1,050 klicks down the rail from Amelia Earhart Skyport, Mother released the pallet from the rail and initiated a two-minute kick thruster burn. At the end of the time, the magnetic iris sliced through the kick thruster's solid fuel stack, cutting off the burn. The pallet with *Gryphon-10* and me headed on a tangent away from the Earth at almost eight km/s on a path that passed forty-seven klicks over Fred Noonan Skyport, over Southern California, and that would intersect the 160-klick orbit on the other side of the Earth. During the acceleration phase, in addition to my leg straps, I could feel the belly band holding me securely in the pod. When the acceleration ceased, and I was in freefall, I still could feel the reassuring pressure of the belly band—kinda like Apryl's legs around my torso on Howland Island just before all this got underway.

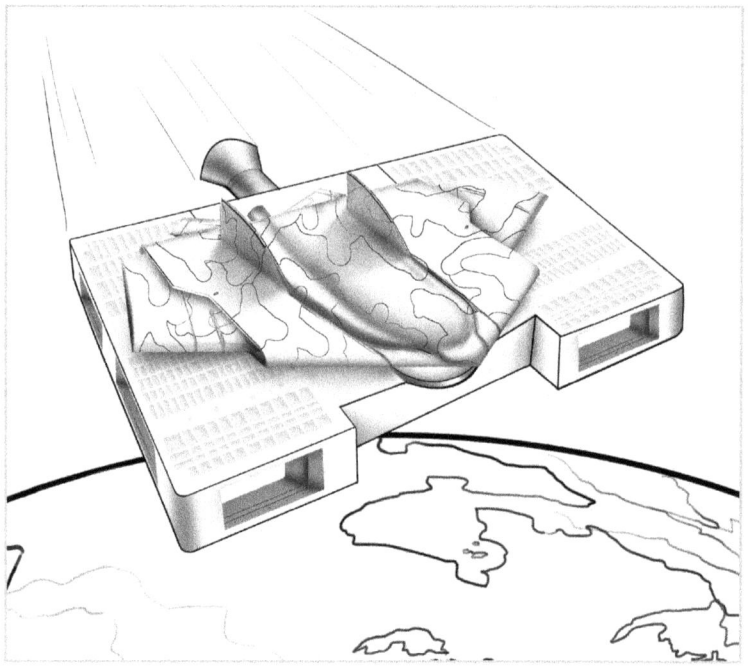

Figure 6—Gryphon and pallet with Tiger Baily approaching LEO.

LEO—MANNED

To put things into perspective, I was in an elliptical orbit with perigee at eighty klicks and apogee at 160 klicks. At apogee on the opposite side of the Earth, Mother would fire the kick thruster to change my orbit from elliptical to circular. When I reached the right point in my orbit, she would rotate the pallet 180° and fire the kick thruster to slow my velocity and separate the *Gryphon-10* from the pallet. I would drop from orbit and then skip into and out of the atmosphere, slowing down each time until I was over San Diego at a manageable height and speed for landing.

As I whipped along my elliptical orbit climbing higher with each passing minute, I had a grand view of the Earth below. "Are you seeing this?" I asked.

"Roger that," Master Chief Boldt responded dryly.

"That's San Diego," I said at thirteen minutes. "Hi down there, guys!"

I told Mother to superimpose borders over my panoramic view, and two minutes later, I crossed over the Oklahoma Panhandle with a cloud cover that made it difficult to see the ground.

"Altitude one-hundred-thirty klicks," Boldt's dry voice informed me.

As I continued to gain altitude, five minutes later, brilliantly lit nighttime Washington, DC, swept below me.

"No time to say Hello—Good-bye…I'm flying through your nighttime sky," I sang, floating in my sling, awestruck by the speed of passing.

"Roger that," the Master Chief opined.

During the ten minutes it took to cross a darkened Atlantic, I watched lightning bolts play between towering thunderheads of a massive storm system creating a magical landscape beneath my flying carpet.

"Good morning Mauritania!" I said in my best Robin Williams imitation as I approached the West African Coast.

"Roger that. Altitude one-hundred-fifty klicks."

In the final ten minutes, I swept southeast across the Gulf of Guinea and passed into the Republic of the Congo.

"Stand by for pallet rotation," the Master Chief advised.

Dawn was breaking as I swept over Brazzaville and crossed the Congo River that bordered the Democratic Republic of the Congo. The sun glinted off the broad river surface as the city lights winked out below. The terminator swept past, and forested landscape turned from dark purple to bright green as the sun washed the blackness from the sky. As I passed over Kinshasa, the Master Chief droned, "One-hundred-sixty klicks."

Mother rotated the pallet to the proper angle and counted down the final five seconds to the circularizing burn: "Five, four, three, two, one… Initiate!"

A bright morning star flared briefly for any of the eleven-million inhabitants of Africa's third-largest city who happened to be looking overhead at that moment.

And that's when all hell broke loose.

LEO—DISASTER

"**W**hat the fuck!" I yelped as the rear of my *Gryphon-10* pallet tilted sharply upward while the nose yawed to the right. Then the whole thing started to corkscrew while the kick thruster continued its burn. I was terrified. Almost without thinking, I manually jettisoned the kick thruster and watched it corkscrew ahead of me until it flared out. I lost it in the glare of the morning sun.

Keeping tight control of my rising panic, and very glad my belly strap held me firmly in the pod, I told Control about my problem while I deployed a tethered holocam to inspect the damage.

As I related earlier, I was in a stable orbit off to the right by 22.5° but had to get control of my tumble.

With the back end of the pallet partially melted, and a large chunk missing from my right fin, Mother gave me the bad news: "Probability of complete structure failure one hundred percent."

"Well…that's not exactly good news," I said, knowing Flight Control was listening.

"Tiger," Master Chief Boldt said, "we're working on that. While you're at it, try to conserve your oxygen."

"Control and Bird, this is Baker Socket, Baxter here. We're checking the backup bird right now. We'll send it up the skytower in about fifteen minutes."

"Baxter, this is Control. Before you send the pallet up, locate four oxygen bottles, and strap them to the pallet. Connect them to a manifold in the center of the back of the pallet. Also, send up oxygen fittings, adaptors, and any tools you think Tiger might need… anything at all." The Master Chief paused. "Oh yeah…two complete TBH boot sets." Then continued more softly. "Remember, the Skipper is up there all alone, he can't get down, and he's running out of oxygen."

"I heard that, Master Chief," I said, feeling a bit more in control. "It's not so bad as all that. Besides, the Senior Chief is already sending me everything I'll need to complete my job up here." As an afterthought, I added, "Ain't that right, Bob?"

All I heard back was a grunt.

"Mother," I said, "how close are you to fixing my tumble?"

"Approaching a solution now," she said. "Are you ready?"

"Go for it!" I said, gripping my handholds with more force than I probably needed, once again glad for the belly strap.

I sensed the nozzle moving on its gimble and felt several short rocket bursts from *Gryphon-10's* thruster—not a lot of pressure on my body, but they did push me around a bit. Mother had no way to fire forward, but somehow she managed to stop both the rotation and wobble with a small net addition to my forward velocity, which meant my orbit had changed from circular to a modest ellipse.

※

I was pretty certain that a lot was happening Earthside that was being kept from me. As the heavens above me ceased their wild gyrations, I really had nothing to do but sightsee. And I gotta tell you, it was some kind of spectacular.

By the time I was on an even keel again, Australia's nighttime west coast was just ahead of me. To the north at Coral Bay, I was told, the Australians were planning to build the Outback Loop, but as I flashed overhead, there was nothing to see of the project, just the twinkling lights of the town.

Four minutes later, as I flashed over the Great Barrier Reef Marine Park, Master Chief Boldt came up on the circuit. "Tiger, we just lifted the backup system to Amelia Earhart Skyport. We're still working out the orbital details, but we're pretty certain we can get the spare to you before you run out of oxygen."

"Thanks, Master Chief. I needed to hear that," I said with a chuckle. I had no doubt that if it were humanly possible, the guys would, at the very least, resupply me with oxygen before I ran out. And if they didn't, well…it was an analog of a parachute not opening.

As I crossed the darkened Equator five minutes later, the Master Chief brought me up to date. "We got the orbital parameters worked out, Tiger.

The backup unit will rendezvous with you at the same location where the shit hit the fan in the first place. Problem is, the time is too tight to do it this orbit. You'll have to complete one more orbit to make sure you and the backup arrive over Kinshasa in exactly the same place at exactly the same time."

I was about to respond back when he added, "Yeah, we know your oxygen is tight. You might want to try breathing every other breath until the rendezvous."

"Thanks a lot, Master Chief. Seriously, what are my options?"

"We're working on that. Stand by."

"Not going anywhere, Master Chief, other than the railroad track I'm riding."

I was approaching the coast of Mexico when Flight Control got back to me. "We're sending Mother parameters to lower your total oxygen content to sixteen percent," Master Chief Boldt told me. "When you move around at all or undertake any exertion, she will boost the percentage to seventeen percent. You'll be fine, and your reduced consumption will give you the added margin you'll need when the backup gets there."

So, that was good news, sort of…it sure beat having to breathe every other breath.

As I came up on North America, my changed orbit was obvious. I passed well south of Baja California, and almost directly over the sixteenth-century town of San Luis Potosi, but it was too dark to see anything, except the lights of the town itself. Before I really had a chance to integrate the lights below me, I flashed past the Mexican coast into the Gulf about five hundred klicks south of Houston.

Houston—home to flight control of virtually every American manned space flight except mine. The phrase *Houston Flight Control* had captured my imagination since I was a small kid. And that's when it hit me.

"Master Chief Boldt, are you still there?" Silly question. Of course, he was.

"What's on your mind, Tiger?"

"Since I probably won't be landing in San Diego, can we arrange to land in the parking lot in front of the entrance to Houston Mission Control?"

I have absolutely no idea what kind of behind-the-scenes activity this innocent proposal generated, but by the time I was coming up on the West Coast of Africa for the second time, Boldt got back to me.

"It's a go, Tiger! NASA loves the idea and will do everything possible to facilitate your landing." The Master Chief actually sounded excited. "We're working out the parameters now. Generally, twenty-one-hundred klicks from Houston, you'll initiate your drop. That's just off the coast of Baja. You'll be able to see it when you initiate.

"Now…let's focus on getting you home." The Master Chief's emotionless voice had returned, so it was back to business.

Mother shifted my oxygen content to sixteen. I could tell the difference, and that made me think. The reason we were doing this is that if we didn't, I would deplete my oxygen supply before I had a chance to hook into the one they were sending me. If I ran out of oxygen before the backup pallet reached me, or even about the time it arrived, I wouldn't have enough brainpower left to do what was necessary. That thought nailed it. I decided to take a nap to remain on sixteen percent as long as I physically could.

LEO—RENDEZVOUS

Master Chief Boldt's voice jolted me awake. "Tiger, Control…Look alive! You've got work to do."

I quickly checked my heads-up readings and the map Mother had superimposed over my panoramic view. I had slept for about an hour, give or take. The backup had been launched and was on its way to our rendezvous. As the Sun rose ahead of me, I passed south of Houston, 12,000 klicks from the meet-up twenty-four minutes hence.

"Tiger, time to do what you practiced in Max."

"I practiced a lot of things in Max…most of them got me killed!" I wasn't really grumpy, but my sense of humor was lagging behind me in orbit.

"Tiger, you need to extricate yourself from the *Gryphon*. Gotta be ready for whatever might happen at rendezvous."

"Roger, Master Chief. I'm working on that right now." Boldt was more than right. If things went exactly as planned, my pallet and the replacement would end up side-by-side. All I would need to do is slip out of the damaged *Gryphon-10* into the replacement, and then ride it out for about forty-three minutes to the drop point. But real life has a habit of interfering with the best-laid plans. I had one shot at the rendezvous. I needed every advantage I could get.

Time to undress. I manually released the seal around the pod cover. A cloud of moisturized air escaped, forming an expanding halo around the pallet. I activated the mechanism that opened the *Gryphon-10* pod cover like a clamshell carrying me with it. My arms and hands were free, so I loosened the waistband and then undid the leg straps. I had nineteen minutes left to think about all the things that could go wrong.

"Tiger, Control…The backup will approach you from below to your rear. Its differential velocity should be very small both along your orbital axis and your vertical axis. You should see it in about five minutes."

"I'm lookin' hard, Master Chief, trust me!"

LEO—MISS

Looking down against the bright Atlantic surface for a small approaching object is not exactly what I had trained for, but you better believe I concentrated more than I ever had before.

I picked it up three or four minutes later—I sort of lost track of time I was concentrating so hard. "I see the pallet, Master Chief!"

"That's a bit early," he answered. "It's gonna go right past you…but pretty slow." He paused. "Give me an angle from the base of your pallet."

I sighted and let Mother do the math. "Ten-and-a-half degrees, Master Chief."

"Yeah, we see it. That's a problem. Should be about seven to eight degrees. Sucker's going to pass you at about one-point-four meters-per-second. What's the pallet's relative bearing drift?"

I watched it for a few seconds. "It's pulling off to my right…"

"Wait one," the Master Chief said. "I'm patching NASA through."

"This is Flight Control Houston, Tiger. We got you and the approaching pallet on high-resolution radar. You are at three-hundred meters and closing at one-point-four meters-per-second, decreasing. At CPA (*that's*

Closest Point of Approach for you landlubbers), the pallet will be one hundred meters off your starboard side at ten-point-four degrees above your plane, one-point-two meters-per-second relative velocity."

"Mother, time of CPA?" I asked.

"Three-minutes-and-fifty-seconds."

I thought about tethering myself to my pallet, but considering the forces involved, I decided I would be better off on my own under TBH propulsion. After all, 1.4 m/sec was about walking speed. I should be able to catch the pallet just a football field away.

"Mother, give me angle and time to commence personal burn to rendezvous with pallet." Believe it or not, she actually understood that.

"Two-minutes-and-three-seconds; heading zero-nine-zero relative; ten-degree up-angle. You will need to correct continuously as you traverse."

I had less than a minute. As Mother counted down the last few seconds, I said, "Captain, Master Chief…wish me luck!" I oriented myself and tapped both big toes…and whispered, *There's no place like home!*

Mother set my heads-up display to show the pallet carrying the spare *Gryphon-10* on its projected path, myself on my projected path, and the rendezvous point. I concentrated on keeping my path intersecting the rendezvous point. I was a little low and to the right. I bent both knees just a bit and moved my left leg outward a fraction. As the points closed, I got ready and then tapped both toes to shut down the TBH boots. As we closed still five meters apart, I tucked and rolled, pointing my feet at the pallet. Two taps with each toe—on and off, and I grabbed the pallet.

"Nice job!" the Master Chief commented. "Now buckle in! You got a circularizing burn coming up in a minute."

He didn't say *Hustle!*, but I heard it in his voice. The *Gryphon-10* was a hardy beast, but it was not designed to take acceleration with the clamshell open. It took me thirty-five seconds to open it, lie face down, and shut it over me. I was not strapped to anything, so I grabbed my hand controls, braced my knees against the pod, and held on.

"On my mark," Master Chief Boldt said. "Three, two, one…fire!"

I don't know what I was expecting, but the acceleration caught me by surprise. About ten seconds or so of something less than one-gee, and that was it.

"You're good to go," the Master Chief informed me.

I couldn't have increased my oxygen percentage to 21% if I had wanted to. I was quite literally on my last couple of breaths. I rolled out of the clamshell and quickly hooked the oxygen manifold to my backpack and recharged my tanks. There was no need to inform Control.

I opened the clamshell and pressed against the pod cover. I strapped my legs to the pod. I tightened the broad waist strap, placed my arms at my sides, and then closed and sealed the *Gryphon-10*. As I crossed the east coast of Africa, I was ready to go.

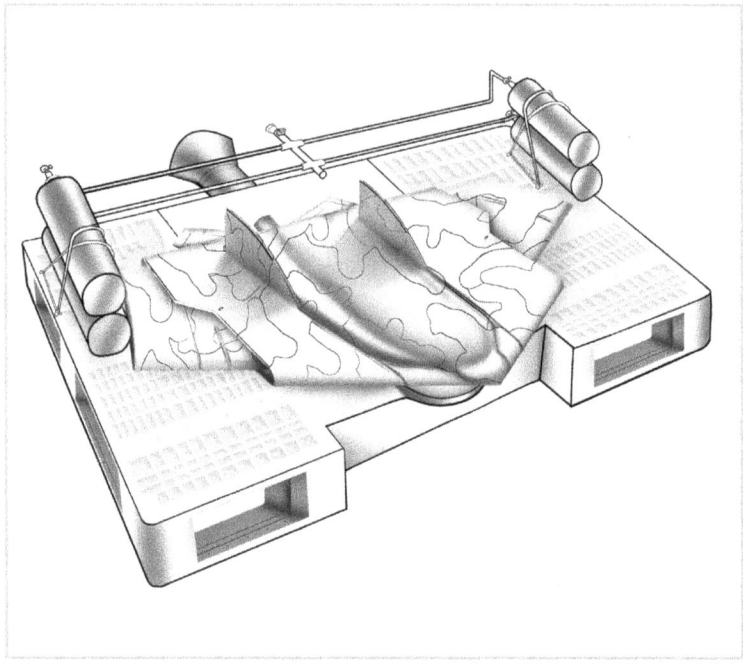

Figure 7—Spare Gryphon on pallet with oxygen tanks and makeshift piping.

LEO—ORBIT SHIFT

By now, I had sufficient oxygen to make several trips around the globe, but my bladder bag was filling, and I had already tested the capacity of my astronaut diapers. It was definitely time to go home.

"Tiger, this is Control." It was the Master Chief again.

"What's up, Master Chief?"

"Nothin ain't easy," he said. "Your successful rendezvous and burn were not *entirely* successful. You can't make Houston on your present path."

"Well…sheeit!" I said. I really wanted to do that landing. "Master Chief," I said after a minute of thought, "check with Houston, but I think we might be able to adjust my orbit. I got a bunch of pressurized oxygen up here with the manifold pointed to the rear. I got the nearly full kick thruster and my TBH boots with two spare sets."

"Well…" Master Chief Boldt was obviously skeptical.

"I can do another orbit or two if we have to. We still have half-a-day before night sets over Houston."

"Tiger, this is Houston Flight Control. I need a complete inventory of what you have up there. SWIC Flight Control, give me the mass and dimension parameters for the items on Tiger's inventory."

My part was easy. "The pallet with a partially used kick thruster; four oxygen tanks, just an RCH under six-hundred-eighty atmospheres; the TBH boots I'm wearing and two fully charged extra pairs; my spacesuit with fully charged pack; the *Gryphon-10* with fully charged thruster." I also listed the hand tools Senior Chief Baxter had attached to the pallet.

"Houston…" It was the Master Chief. "I'm calling you on a secure line."

I knew what this was all about. NASA is a sieve when it comes to classified material, and *Gryphon-10* carried a classification above Top Secret. Capt. Nelson would be bending some ears at NASA to ensure the confidentiality of our project.

At SWIC headquarters, all available personnel assembled in the North Island hanger. They had one purpose, one goal: quickly create a mockup of my pallet and link it to NASA by holocam. Our best and NASA's best people would be working with the mockup to find a real-time solution to my predicament.

It took them a bit over a half-hour. They uploaded instructions for Mother and walked me through my part of the operation.

I shifted my oxygen backup to the outside right tank. I modified the oxygen manifold so that by opening just one valve, 680 atm of oxygen would provide thrust to the rear of the pallet, and I attached a stiff wire to the valve handle that reached to my left-hand location outside the carapace. I replaced my TBH boots with a fresh pair and prepared to angle myself with my feet pointing in a direction specified by Mother, varying the angle in real-time as she directed. The combined team decided not to employ the kick thruster because I would need it for deorbiting. They decided not to use the *Gryphon-10's* thruster, but to hold it in reserve for my drop. That was fine by me.

To sum up, I would use thrust generated by the oxygen tanks and whatever my TBH boots would produce. As I came up to a point about 500 klicks northwest of Jarvis Island, I would initiate the "burn" to shift my orbit left by a couple of degrees. The exact time, duration, and direction of thrust would be determined in real-time by Houston's Flight Control Computer, talking directly with Mother.

I had about a half-hour to worry about what would happen if this maneuver didn't work. Worst-case scenario would find me ditching somewhere in the Gulf of Mexico, with rescue coming by air or sea, depending on how far from civilization I hit the drink. Did I say *worst-case-scenario*? Actually, I could think of several that were much worse, but being an optimist, I chose not to consider *not making it* as an option.

My personal time sense must have been out of kilter, because what seemed a minute or so later, Mother announced five minutes to the correction.

I remained inside the *Gryphon-10*, but with the seal cracked and the wire in my hand. Mother had already changed the pallet orientation, so we were pointed about 10° to the left of our direction of travel. Houston had calculated the expected amount of thrust the oxygen bottles would generate, but there were way too many variables to be certain. I was prepared to extract myself from the *Gryphon-10* on a moment's notice to add the thrust of my TBH boots to our acceleration profile.

Mother commenced her countdown: "Ten, nine… three, two, one…fire!"

I pulled the wire, and wouldn't you know, it slipped from the valve handle without opening the valve. "Fuck it all!" I said while I slid out of the carapace. With my left hand, I grabbed a carabiner with a two-meter safety line attached to my utility belt and slapped it onto a tie-down to the left of the wingsuit while I swung back to the manifold and twisted the valve with my right. A stream of oxygen looking every bit like a small rocket exhaust shot out the hole in the manifold. The pallet shot forward, popping the *Gryphon-10* pod cover open and jerking my utility belt, dragging me behind the pallet with a pull that had to be approaching one-gee.

If the acceleration damaged the *Gryphon*-10 hinge, I might not make it back. I tried to pull myself hand-over-hand along the safety line, but the acceleration was too strong. I had only one option: I tapped both toes. The TBH boots didn't cancel out the acceleration, but they gave me enough advantage to do the hand-over-hand thing. Even so, it took me several seconds. When I got to the pod cover, I tapped my toes to shut down the jets, wrapped a loop of safety line over the open upper end, pulled it down, and cinched it to a tie-down on the other side. Then I held on for the duration.

Finally, Mother ordered, "Secure the burn."

I knew what she meant and didn't argue her terminology. Without letting the safety line go, I reached back and shut the valve. The stream of oxygen dissipated, and everything seemed to return to normal. I unwrapped the safety line from the pod cover and carefully exercised the hinge. So far as I could tell, there was no damage.

As I removed and stowed the safety line, I queried: "What's the status, Master Chief? Did we make it, or am I going to tread water in the Gulf?"

"This is Houston Flight Control, Tiger. We do not fully understand your *Gryphon-10* parameters, but your new orbit passes directly over Trinity Bay."

"That's a go," Master Chief Boldt said without formally identifying himself. "By damn, that's a go!"

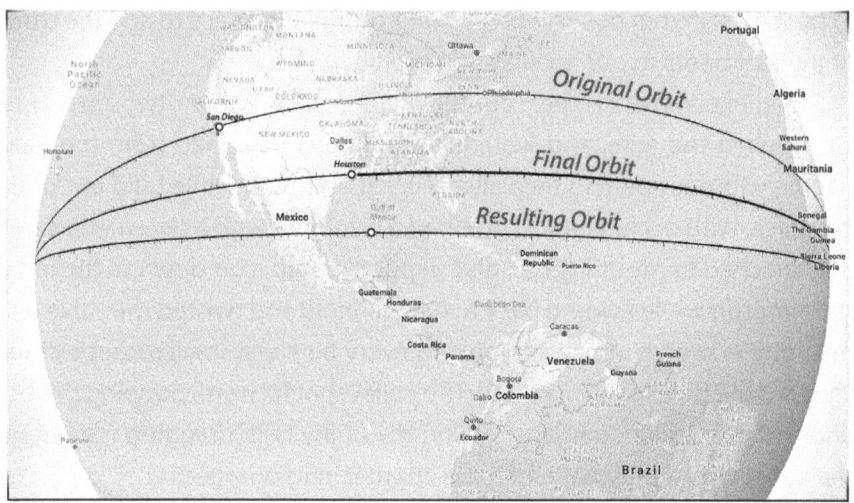

Figure 8—Orbital paths as they pass over the U.S. and Mexico of the Original Orbit, the Resulting Orbit after the accident, and the Final Orbit following the correction.

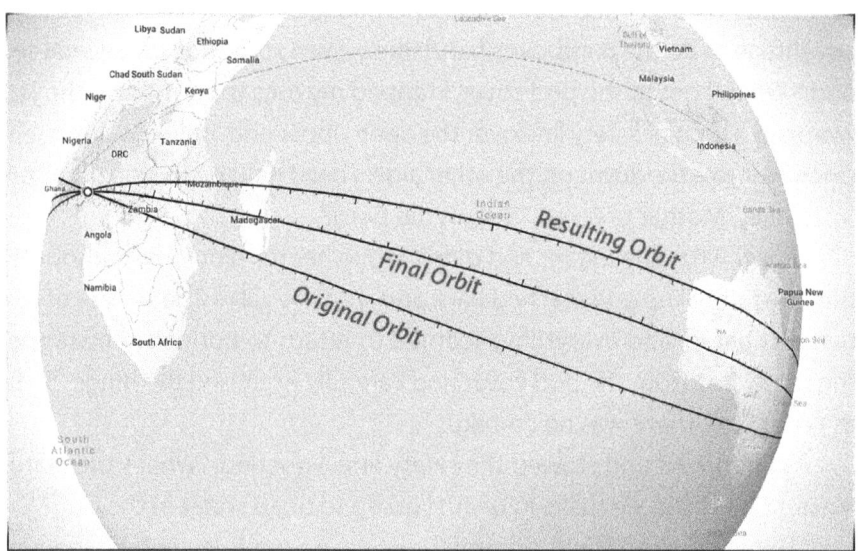

Figure 9—Orbital paths from Kinshasa to Australia of the Original Orbit, the Resulting Orbit after the accident, and the Final Orbit following the correction.

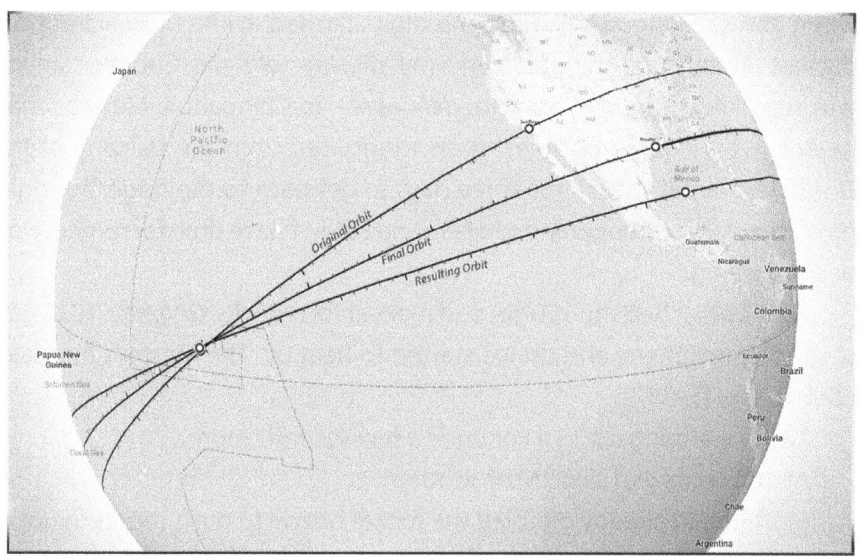

Figure 10—Orbital paths over the Pacific of the Original Orbit, the Resulting Orbit after the accident, and the Final Orbit following the correction over the Pacific.

LEO—MANNED DROP

The first thing Mother did was rotate the pallet 180° with the launch pouch gyro while I secured myself into the *Gryphon*-10. This was the real thing. Once Mother initiated the deorbiting burn, there was no turning back. My heads-up display told me I was 400 klicks off Baja California. I knew the burn would commence right around 200 klicks—I had about thirty seconds.

"Godspeed!" Master Chief Boldt said as Mother initiated the burn twenty-eight seconds later.

After the two longest minutes of my life, Mother cut the kick thruster and rotated everything back, so I was pointed in my direction of travel. I felt a sharp jolt.

"Pallet separation," Mother announced. "Forward velocity six-eight-hundred meters-per-second."

I think I may have briefly seen the pallet fall away, but *Gryphon-10* was heading toward the horizon at 6,800 m/sec while accelerating toward the ocean at 9.8 m/sec^2. Fat chance I actually saw it. Mother had set a timer when she separated the pallet. The digits flashed at the right side of my display. At the two-minute mark, my display told me Copper Canyon was sixty klicks below—*Barranca del Cobre*—in Chihuahua, Mexico. I had been there a couple of times, even wingsuited from the balcony of the Divisadero Hotel. It took me three days to get back to the ridge. But right now, things were happening too fast, and I didn't have time for reminiscing or sightseeing.

As I approached the 150-second mark at forty klicks, *Gryphon-10* began to grab atmosphere, and things started to heat up. The Master Chief said, "Talk to me, Tiger!"

"Suit's warming up…I'll continue a few seconds more…"

At 160 seconds, I said, "Now, Mother!"

Mother had already gimbled the rocket nozzle to push the stern down and adjusted the wing torque controls to optimize my return to space. I felt weight return as I rocketed upward. Then Mother cut the burn and announced, "Forward velocity five-zero-eight-five meters-per-second, net forward transfer nine-two-one kilometers."

I watched the timer reset as Mother said, "Vertical motion zero on my mark…Mark!"

Although Mach numbers don't really matter at this altitude, we started out at Mach 20, and as we began to grab air sixty-four klicks above Copper Canyon, we were still near Mach 18 and frigging hot. When Mother fired the rocket at forty klicks and made slight adjustments to *Gryphon-10's* control surfaces, the wingsuit headed back out of the atmosphere, but 1,500 m/sec slower. We were down to Mach 15 as we commenced the second dip.

Other than the landscape below, I really could tell no meaningful difference between the first and second dips. We hit Mach 9 sixty-five klicks above Big Bend off to my left a bit. After we climbed back out of the atmosphere, we were down to Mach 5, and I let out a whoop.

"You okay?" Boldt wanted to know.

"Yeah! This is cool stuff. I think I could do this without Mother's assistance. The heat tells you when to pop, and physics does everything else."

"Roger that," the Master Chief said, "but Mother will get you to your destination. Without her, you could end up anywhere."

He was right, of course. But I had this thing down…I knew it in my bones.

The next drop put me at forty klicks altitude, 100 klicks west of Houston at sixty m/sec.

Immediately, I was in familiar territory, no different really from my Fred Noonan Skyport jump, except there was land below instead of water.

"Are you guys getting this?" I asked with a level of excitement that even I could hear.

"Piece of cake, Tiger," the Master Chief drawled. "Nothin' you ain't done before. Keep the chatter comin'!"

At this altitude and speed, I had virtually full control of *Gryphon-10*. I brought myself as horizontal as possible and headed for Trinity Bay.

※

"What's the air traffic situation?" I asked.

"NASA'S dealing with that," the Master Chief said.

As he spoke, two NASA jets pulled up, about 200 meters off each side. Even though they couldn't see my face, each pilot gave me a friendly salute.

"Air traffic is being kept away from your path," The Master Chief told me. "Come in about a thousand meters above Trinity Bay, and then follow Mother's display." Then the Master Chief added, "Oh yeah, we've cleared the parking lot for you."

Shouldn't have been necessary, really, I thought. *The* Gryphon-10 *fits in a standard parking lot driveway, but why not.*

As I arrived about a thousand meters above central Trinity Bay, my escorts departed with a wing-waggle. I turned left, and Mother laid out a perfectly clear path right to Houston Flight Control's front door. I was still twenty-eight klicks out, but my path was straight in. I was doing about thirty m/sec, or about 100 km/hr. At that speed, it would take me fifteen minutes, but I would hit the ground half-way there unless I used my booster. And then I had to slow down to walking speed for my landing.

HOUSTON FLIGHT CONTROL—LANDING

With full tanks, I could go a hundred horizontal klicks on the booster. I had only about a quarter of my fuel left, but that was more than sufficient to travel the remaining twenty-eight klicks. This was going to be fun.

I hit the booster for a few seconds while shedding altitude, glided for a bit, and gave it another boost. I was 500 meters away from the parking lot and 100 meters above the trees. A small welcoming crowd stood at the door and across the lot two lanes away. That's when the landing skid of a local news chopper clipped my right fin.

"Where the fuck did that guy come from?" I yelped as I began to lose control of the *Gryphon-10*. A hundred meters is a long way to fall. People scattered in all directions, seeking cover.

"Mother, can you compensate?" I asked.

Mother immediately ignited the booster and drove me skyward for a hundred meters while she experimented with different wing and fin control settings until she found a combination that seemed to work.

"Bring me down in front of the main door," I told Mother.

"This one?" She illuminated the entrance on my display.

"Yeah, that one," I said.

As I slowly spiraled down, the crowd moved closer. I was still about two meters above the pavement moving forward at about one m/sec when a bicycle inexplicably pushed through the crowd directly below me. I don't know what that NASA nerd was thinking, but it was pretty obvious that—even though his head was in the clouds—he had not seen me. I could do absolutely nothing except pull my nose up sharply while retracting my tail.

The *Gryphon-10* is supposed to land on its belly. I didn't do that. I was retracting my tail when I struck the pavement with my booster and fell forward right on top of the rider. I think that was the first indication he had that I was there.

The rider tumbled to the left as his bike flew to the right. He staggered to his feet, staring at the *Gryphon-10* in utter astonishment. As he picked himself up from the pavement, I unsealed the carapace, and the pod cover flipped to vertical, carrying me with it. Still in my spacesuit, I unstrapped myself, stepped away from the *Gryphon-10*, and released my transparent helmet, and then held out my hand to the cyclist. He looked me over in total disbelief, and then removed his helmet and shook my hand.

The crowd cheered, and everyone rushed me, clapping me on the back, shaking my hand, and even kissing me—yep, I got three very welcoming kisses from three more than passable ladies who probably each had more brains than my entire SWIC-3 command combined.

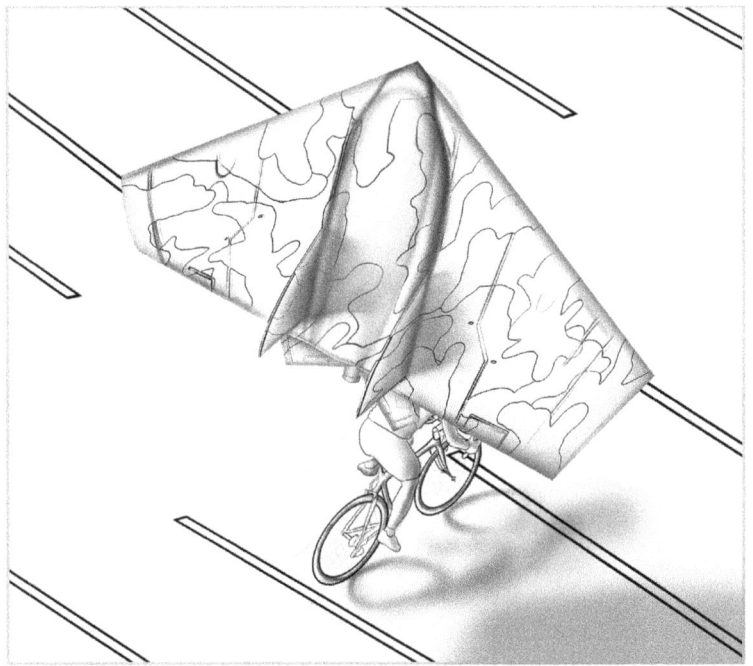

Figure 11—Gryphon with Tiger Baily about to crash into an unaware bike rider.

DAEDALUS LEO—FINALE

Secrets will out, and this one did—rather quickly. I spent a bit of quality time with one of the kissers. The cyclist and I tossed a couple of brews. NASA flew *Gryphon-10* and me back to San Diego where we all celebrated again.

I'm sure you know the rest of the story. Obviously, I survived, and then I survived my second fifteen minutes of fame. My *Gryphon-10* hangs alongside my old *Gryphon-7* in the Smithsonian, but you know that, as well.

Every SWIC-3 team member has now accomplished an LEO drop—without NASA's help, by-the-way. Right now, we're working on a group drop that will simulate dropping into a combat zone. I'll let you know when that finally happens.

DAEDALUS SQUAD
SWIC Squad Drop from Low Earth Orbit

Chapter Three

CHAPTER THREE

DAEDALUS SQUAD

8,000 METERS ABOVE DEATH VALLEY

"What the fuck was that?" someone yelled. It sounded like Jerico Rodriguez—a bit of Hispanic twang. Then I heard a loud crunch as my heads-up display went crazy.

"Shit!" I yelped as my hardshell wingsuit commenced rolling hard to the right. Mother automatically torqued my wings to compensate but without much success. I activated my hypergolic rocket, but nothing happened.

I cleared the alarms in my heads-up display and moved them to the right corner. I could see my squad in formation behind me as I lost altitude on a rolling plunge from 8,000 meters. Chief Douglas Slade's blip moved above my position.

"You got a hole the size of Cappy's head in your right wing," he said, referring to Petty Officer First Class Ronald Caplan. "You ain't got no UDMH left."

"Tell me about it," I muttered.

"I got a problem here, Control," I said, trying to keep my voice steady. I briefly described my situation. "I need some immediate help to get out of this."

CORONADO—SAN DIEGO—SEVERAL DAYS EARLIER

Derek "Tiger" Baily again. I suspect you remember my base jump from Fred Noonan Skyport and my LEO drop, or you wouldn't be reading this. Have you seen *Gryphon-7* and *Gryphon-10* hanging in the Smithsonian Atrium? They're a bit worse for wear but pretty cool to look at.

I'm still with the Teams—the U.S. Navy SEALS, and continue to command SEAL Winged Insertion Command Three, SWIC-3 for short. The way things are in the military right now, I'm probably stuck with my present rank, Lieutenant-Commander.

We were about to do a proof-of-concept LEO drop with an abbreviated 6-man squad using *Gryphon-10 Mk 4s*. I took the lead on this one, pushing my 1st Squad Leader, Lt. Roger Brook, down into the ranks displacing Petty Officer Clyde Horseman, much to Cowboy's displeasure. Cowboy, as everybody called him, along with Petty Officers Benjamin Williams and Christopher Pigwell—Benny and Piggy to the squad, were on standby in case something went wrong.

CORONADO—GRYPHON-10, MK 4

Gryphon-10 Mk 4 looked exactly like the wingsuit I used for the first LEO drop. It differed in subtle ways, however, because of improvements we developed as I and each of my guys made several LEO drops gaining experience and proficiency along the way.

Beyond that, since we intended to use the Gryphon in combat, we incorporated the latest model of a very efficient, hand-held, pulsed energy weapon into a node in the leading edge of either the left or right wing. Its power source is a lightweight BatCap, a unique marriage of a 3-D battery and a thin, large-surface-area flexible capacitor that the SWIC member wears on his back. The capacitor supports twenty rapid-release lethal laser bursts and recharges in less than a minute from the 3-D battery, or it can continuously support a lethal laser burst every five seconds. The 3-D battery needs recharging every five thousand bursts. Before opening the carapace after landing, the SWIC member retrieves the weapon from its node and holsters it just like a sidearm.

Launch pallet improvements ensured that nobody had to go through what happened to me on my first LEO drop. Each pallet carried four tanks. Two were HP oxygen used by the flyer until *Gryphon* separation, attached to the wingsuit with breakaway connectors. The other two carried hypergolic fuel, UDMH and nitrogen tetroxide, for the small hypergolic maneuvering jets that would allow us to get into formation and maintain our pattern until we dropped. Each SWIC-3 team member had completed five LEO drops. Every one of us reached a level of confidence and proficiency as we dealt with problems and solved them on the fly, so to speak. We were as ready as possible for the next step, making a coordinated drop from LEO and landing together at a designated spot on the planet in preparation for doing it for real under combat conditions.

That is, of course, if things went according to plan.

What we were attempting, at least in principle, was straightforward. The six of us would launch in sequence from Amelia Earhart Skyport. Mother would coordinate our detaching from the rail into Hohmann Transfer Orbits (HTO) so that we would find ourselves in a tight group when we reached LEO. From there, at the proper time, we would drop together, again coordinated by Mother, finally landing at our destination, ready to discard our wingsuits to carry out our assigned ground mission or, for that matter, to carry them with us on our backs.

CORONADO—MAX

Max, our full-scale simulator, played a significant role in our preparation. We didn't have the budget for six Max simulators, so we set Max up to simulate a drop of six *Gryphon-10s* with one person at a time in the driver's seat. Each of us ran the Max squad-simulation dozens of times. I did the first run and actually landed the entire squad without a problem. I guess Max was being easy on me because I crashed and burned big-time on my second run. With practice, we all became so proficient that in the end, Max was not able to crash any of us. Remember, however, that Max was only as good as his programming. We entered virtually every kind of possible contingency we could think of, and Max threw every one of them at each of us, singly and in various combinations. Too bad we were not a bit more imaginative thinking up possible things that could go wrong.

Just like on my first LEO drop, however, everything we did up to this point was theoretical, *everything*. As before, we not only gave Max every scrap of reentry information we could find, but Max also had everything we had generated with our many LEO drops since then. Max already had everything we knew about upper atmosphere weather and every bit of physics that could possibly bear on the problem. Mother knew everything Max knew and was connected to worldwide live feeds. In our real drop, Mother would know everything possible about the path ahead, and everything Max had done in similar situations during simulation runs. Mother would have every possible edge to give us the desired outcome. Yet…until we actually made the first squad drop, all we had were numbers that we hoped made sense.

CORONADO—SQUAD DROP PREP

We had reached a level of experience and proficiency so that we no longer set up a backup unit for each of our drops. As always, each man was ultimately responsible for his own *Gryphon*. Before we loaded the six units on the waiting Navy jet transport, Master Chief Boldt and I inspected each unit, carefully and completely. Then each team member inspected his own unit again. This was the big one—failure was not an option.

Capt. Nelson maintained his high-level discussions with his Team boss. On this morning, Capt. Nelson informed me that the White House would be watching on an encrypted holobroadcast. Apparently, the Commander-in-Chief was a frustrated wingsuit flyer wannabe.

HOWLAND & BAKER ISLANDS—PRELAUNCH

I departed Coronado for North Island Airfield with Senior Chief Baxter and the entire First Squad plus three guys from Second Squad. I wanted one man assisting each flyer with the Senior Chief in charge. We were pretty busy, and I don't remember saying anything witty as I had done on our departure for the first LEO drop. I do recall thinking that this would be a piece of cake. Good thing I didn't say that out loud, as it turned out.

Trips to Howland Island on the Navy supersonic transport were becoming pretty routine. This one was no different. We jetted down the runway, lifted through sparse clouds into a brilliant blue stratosphere, leaving a layer of puffy cirrocumulus clouds far below us. We turned toward Hawaii as we accelerated to nearly Mach 2.

I slept right through our refueling stop in Hawaii, waking up as we rolled to a stop at Amelia Earhart International Airport under a blistering equatorial sun. As if they were greeting my return, thousands of sooty terns, lesser frigatebirds, and masked boobies filled the sky, kept clear of aircraft by built-in sonic systems.

Apryl Searson met me at the ramp, her pixie blond hair, and thin, short dress fluttering in the tropical breeze. She took my arm and walked me to the Launch Loop International (LLI) Howland headquarters building, where she had already prepared an appropriate place to greet me properly. By now, these trysts were legendary in SWIC, but none of the guys begrudged me my good fortune. Actually, the pickings were sufficiently slim and the schedule so tight, that they really had no chance.

At the end of the tarmac, LLI's two Chinooks waited with cargo bays open, twin rotors seemingly wilting in the hot tropical sun. Senior Chief Baxter and his six guys unloaded the six pallets with help from Lt. Brook and the other flyers and then loaded two into the Chinooks. They all accompanied the first two pallets to Baker. And then returned for two more, and then for the remaining two.

※

I spent a few minutes with Sam Davidson, the local LLI Director, bringing him up to date on what we were doing. He had been following our activities closely, and probably was as anxious as the rest of us for the success of this next step. Now that the Atlantic Launch Loop was in operation, Slingshot had a bit less pressure on its 24/7 schedule of throwing people and cargo into space. No matter how you cut it, though, Sam was launching 2,000 metric tons of cargo and eighty personnel capsules into space every day.

"Where is all that stuff going, Sam?" I asked as I stood to leave.

"Out there," Sam said with a grin gesturing toward the ceiling and slapped my back, something that was becoming a ritual. "Good luck, Tiger! Like I've told you each time we meet like this, I'm glad it's you, and not me."

※

This time around, Apryl accompanied me to Baker Island in the last Chinook. Senior Chief Baxter joined us. Even with the pallet, the three of us had plenty of room. The rest of the guys had crowded around the pallet in the other Chinook.

"Nice to see you, Miss Apryl," Baxter said, his eyes twinkling.

"And you, Senior Chief," Apryl said, kissing his cheek as he blushed crimson. Apryl giggled, kissed him again, and snuggled back beside me.

After we landed at Baker, Apryl and I, accompanied by the other five flyers, took the five-minute trip in a personnel capsule up to Amelia Earhart Skyport. Meanwhile, under Senior Chief Baxter's supervision, the articulating boom crane loader hoisted the pallets over the rail, where a crew member attached each to a launch dolly. The process had become pretty routine, but the Senior Chief never let his attention wander during the loading.

AMELIA EARHART SKYPORT—PRELAUNCH

At Amelia Earhart Skyport, our capsule tilted to horizontal, sealed against the skyport lock, and the door opened inward. Apryl and I stepped into the reception area, followed by my guys. The capsule closed behind us, and the lock sealed. Apryl took a seat against the outer wall, and I addressed my team.

"You've all done this before, but individually. Anything happens like it did with Cappy or me, you got more to think of than yourself. We're back to being a team, a fighting team—even though this is just a drill." I got a chuckle from the five in front of me. "Know your position in the formation at all times. If a teammate gets into trouble and you can help, do so! But don't risk everyone in the process. Remember, with this exercise, we're showing the mucky-mucks that SWIC is a viable insertion tool, perhaps the best we've ever developed."

"Hooyah!" Chief Slade responded, joined by the rest, me included, "Hooyah!"

"Okay, guys, suit up!" Slade ordered, and a minute or so later, the first pallet arrived.

With skytower traffic stopped, all the guys except me hustled through the personnel lock. They removed the fairing and stowed it, and then they prepped the pallet with its *Gryphon* payload, swinging the wingsuit pod cover to vertical on its hinges like a clamshell. Slade examined every part of the pallet and wingsuit. He was quick but efficient, mindful of the queued-up freight pallets and passenger capsules waiting down at Baker Socket. As he finished, he signaled Lt. Roger Brook to do his final system check. Rog, as we called him, had looked over Slade's shoulder through his entire system check, so he was certain that everything was ready, but he still went through the list just to make sure.

Rog stepped up on his *Gryphon*, backed against the carapace cover, and one of the guys secured his legs and torso and lowered him into the wingsuit.

"Time to go," I said to Apryl, who was snuggled against me on the same couch we used before my first LEO drop. The Milky Way, that multi-colored diamond-studded bracelet spanning the sky, was as awesome as ever, taking my breath away as I untangled myself from Apryl.

Apryl kissed me passionately. "Be safe, Tiger…I worry about you."

Of course, we had no idea what lay before me.

※

I suited up quickly. Our lightweight suits incorporated high-pressure oxygen bottles, electronic carbon-dioxide scrubbers, and TBH jet boots that slipped over the suit feet and calves.

I stepped through the personnel lock onto the dock just as Rog's pallet disappeared around the bend to receive kick thruster and launch dolly. The second pallet arrived, followed almost immediately by a personnel capsule carrying Baxter and his crew. They disembarked into the Skyport lounge where they suited up and joined us on the dock as Chief Douglas's pallet queued up at the end of the dock. We had room for three pallets in queue before we had to launch the first. We generally knew the sequence, but Mother would coordinate the entire operation, based upon the time of the first launch, the times of each subsequent inspection and launch, and when each pallet was released to its specific HTO. The biggest potential variable was how long it took to inspect each pallet, load the flyer, and put him in the queue.

We had practiced the sequence often enough back in Coronado so that we actually worked like an oiled machine. I say *we*, but that's not quite fair. It was the guys under Senior Chief Baxter's watchful eye who pulled it off. Even though I commanded SWIC-3, up there, right then, I was just an observant passenger.

Petty Officer First Class Francisco Rodriguez—Jerico, for some unknown reason—conducted his inspection and was snugged into his *Gryphon*. His pallet joined the queue.

Next up, Petty Officer First Class Ronald Caplan. Cappy, as the guys called him, had already experienced one mishap during LEO drops. From his perspective, this drop had to be perfect. His inspection lasted somewhat longer than the others, but that was fine—no one begrudged him the extra time. Baxter looked at me even though it wasn't necessary. Up here, he was in charge. I nodded, and he signaled to launch Rog down the rail, making room for Cappy's pallet.

Petty Officer Second Class Peter Farwall was next, and I followed Pete. Like Cappy, I inspected my pallet and *Gryphon* with extra care. I certainly didn't want any problems this time.

I stepped onto the pallet, backed up against the pod cover, and allowed the crew to strap me in; the process almost felt normal. Then the crew swung down the pod cover and me, sealed the edges all around, pressurized it, and checked for leaks. The gantry moved me to the end of the queue while Pete received his kick thruster and launch dolly.

AMELIA EARHART SKYPORT—LAUNCH

"Control, this is Tiger—comm check," I said as I felt the kick thruster attach.

"Loud and clear, Tiger," Master Chief Boldt responded. "Just like old times." As always, his calm voice was reassuring.

"Mother, state your status," Boldt ordered.

"Rog, Slade, Jerico, Cappy, and Pete are down the rail. Rog and Slade are in HTO. Standing by to launch Tiger. You," she added as an afterthought. Mother's voice was business-like but still had a soothing, contralto tone.

"Ready when you are," Boldt said.

I felt the gantry lower my pallet to the rail. I was snug as a caterpillar inside my Gryphon cacoon. It felt warm and comfortable

"On my count," Master Chief Boldt said. "Five, four, three, two, one… Launch!"

SLINGSHOT RAIL

As I surged forward, I reminded myself that this was my sixth time down the rail. Staying relaxed, even in tough circumstances, has always come easy to me. By now, this was a piece of cake, except my right buttock started to itch. My arms were free to move inside the *Gryphon* wings, but try as hard as I might, I couldn't reach the itch. I finally moved my rump up against the carapace cover and wiggled. Getting that itch was blessed relief.

Exactly four minutes and ten seconds after launch, Mother rotated my pallet 30° to the left. Thirty-three seconds later and 1,328 klicks down the rail from Amelia Earhart Skyport, Mother released my pallet from the rail and initiated a two-minute-fifteen-second kick thruster burn. At the end of that time, the magnetic iris sliced through the kick thruster's solid fuel stack, cutting off the burn. The pallet with me in my *Gryphon* headed on a path away from the Earth at almost 8 km/s on a path that passed 290 klicks to the north and 19 klicks above Fred Noonan Skyport, and that would intersect the 160 klick orbit on the other side of the Earth at the same point and same time the other five converged. When the acceleration ceased, I relaxed into freefall, fondly remembering Apryl's ministrations in the LLI Admin Building on Howland Island and her Skyport-kiss just before I suited up.

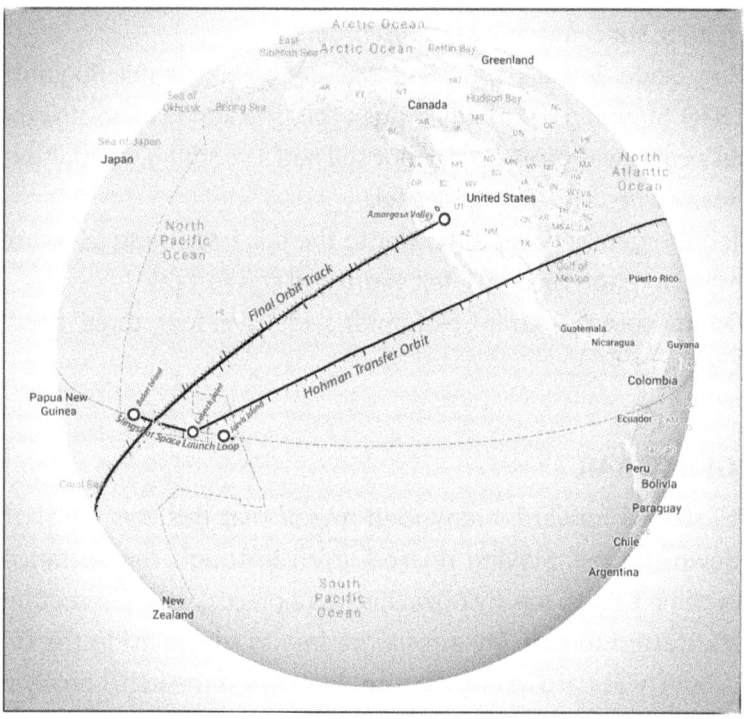

Figure 12—Slingshot Space Launch Loop with the Hohmann Transfer Orbit and the last leg of the final orbit track from Australia to the final landing at Amargosa Valley.

LEO

By now, this was old hat. I was in an elliptical HTO with perigee at 80 klicks and apogee at 160 klicks—just like the other five times. The one big difference, however, is that when I reached apogee on the opposite side of the Earth, the rest of my team would be clustered together waiting for me—at least that was the plan.

Time to determine the status and get things organized. "Control, this is Tiger…status of rendezvous," I requested.

"Rog and Slade are at the assembly point," Mother answered. "Jerico is approaching, arrival in twelve minutes. Cappy is eighteen minutes out, Pete is twenty-five minutes out, and you are thirty-nine minutes out."

Do you have any idea how long thirty-nine minutes can be? I remembered sitting on a small stool in my mother's kitchen as a four-year-old watching the wall clock. My mother had said that we would leave when the big hand reached twelve. Those forty minutes took forever, but these thirty-nine minutes took even longer. And to complicate the matter, that itch came back. At least, this time, I knew how to fix it. The upside of this wait was that I had time to admire the Earth below.

On each set of LEO drops, we had set ourselves on different orbital paths, landing twice in the US, once in Africa, once in Australia, and one water-landing near the Soloman Islands in the South Pacific. This time we were following our original orbit fairly closely, planning on landing together in the Amargosa Valley 145 klicks northwest of Vegas.

As I climbed higher along my HTO, while I played tag with my itch, I had a grand view of the Earth below, but I no longer felt compelled to give Control a blow-by-blow show-and-tell. Baja was covered with clouds, but I knew it was below because Mother had superimposed a map over my heads-up display. Amazingly, Laguna de Myrán, half-way between the Pacific and Atlantic in central Mexico, was filled with water for the first time in years. A swirling tropical storm system off New Orleans made me happy that was not my destination. For a change, the Atlantic was about as empty of cloud cover as it ever gets, giving me a grand view of horizon-to-horizon ocean blue until I ran into the terminator about half-way across. I crossed the African coast just south of Mauritania heading toward Lagos, Nigeria's largest city, already a shining diamond on the nighttime horizon.

As I approached Lagos below me, my heads-up display showed my five companions up ahead and above, waiting patiently for my arrival.

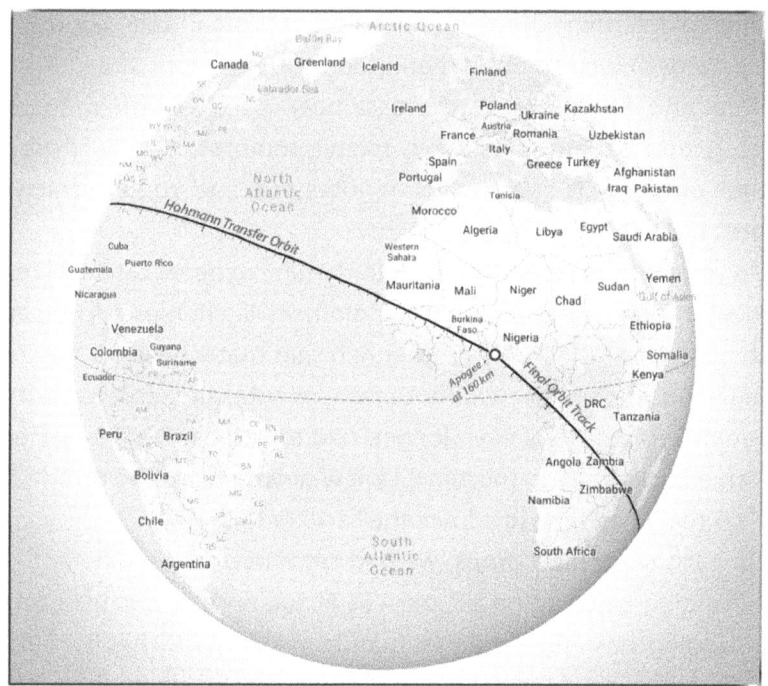

Figure 13—Hohmann Transfer Orbit to the apogee over Lagos. Final circularized orbit track from apogee.

"Squad, this is Tiger. I'm on approach, five minutes out."

"Tiger, this is Rog...we see you in heads-up. You're not yet physically visible. Are your red-green flashers on?"

"They are," I answered, and then I was able to pick out their five sets of flashers against the stars. "I have visible on you," I said.

"I will park you fifty meters below the formation," Mother interrupted. "Stand by for circularizing burn."

Mother ignited the kick thruster for a few seconds—thank goodness nothing went wrong this time. I rubbed my buttock against the carapace cover as I checked my heads-up. The five team members were arrayed above me in a triangular formation with the point missing. That was my slot. Twelve meters separated each pallet horizontally, and three meters vertically. Slade and Jerico filled row two above and behind point, and Cappy, Rog, and Pete made up row three above and behind row two.

Using my maneuvering jets, I brought my pallet to the point position ahead of and three meters below Slade and Jerico. I could have let Mother do this, but I thought it was a great opportunity to show off a bit. We were ready to go.

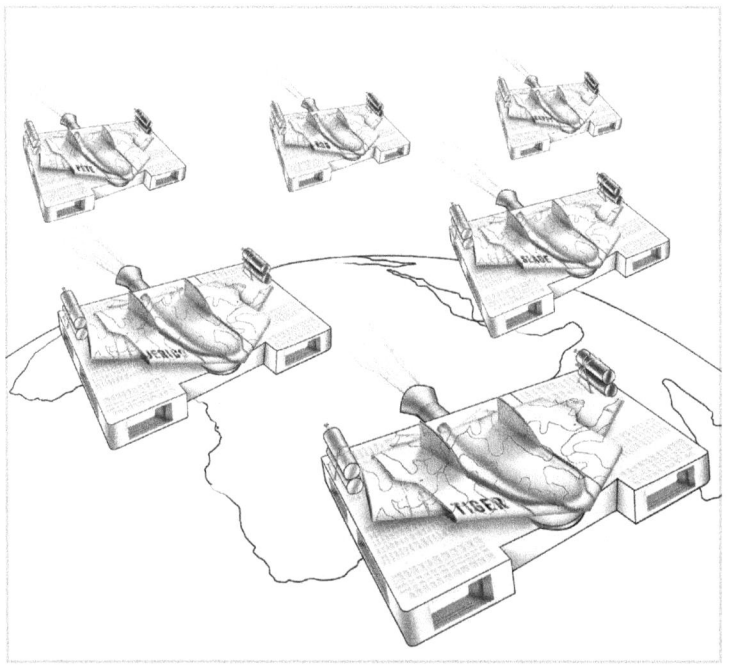

Figure 14— Tiger Baily's SWIC team on pallets in LEO with spare oxygen and fuel tanks.

LEO—SQUAD DROP

"Mother, update status," I ordered.

"Fifty-two minutes until squad drop," she answered.

"Control, this is Tiger. I'm going to do the one-eighty now while we're hanging loose."

"Roger that, Tiger. Let Mother handle it."

And she did. Synchronously, Mother rotated all six pallets with their gyros. I watched the eerie dance on my heads-up. If I hadn't known better, I would have taken it for a video game.

"Everybody good?" I asked casually, knowing that my guys were focused—perhaps too much since we were still forty-five minutes to the drop.

"Rog, good!"

"Slade, okay!"

"Jerico, A-OK, Boss!"

"Cappy is fine!"

"Pete, too!"

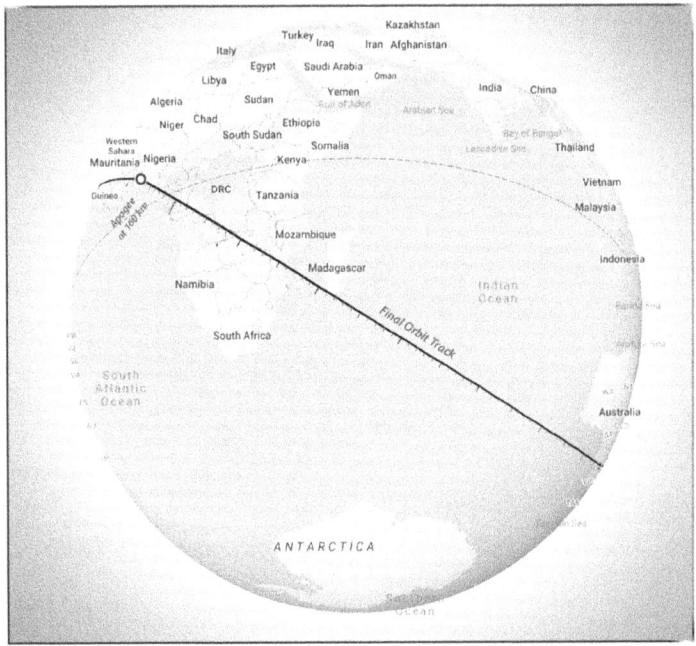

Figure 15—Final orbit track over the Indian Ocean to Australia.

Ten minutes later, we met the morning terminator as we passed south of Madagascar, its visible southern tip brown and dry, rising out of the deep blue ocean to the north.

"Let's drop down there and take us a vacation," Jerico said. "Never been there…looks like an interesting place."

"Too late for this orbit," Cappy quipped. "Gotta go around again and commence our drop over western Zimbabwe."

"Might not be welcome there," Pete said. "I hear they don't like people like us…"

"Cut the chatter!" Chief Slade snapped.

Seventeen minutes of empty Indian Ocean later, except for some streaky clouds that looked like they were trying to form a tropical storm, we crossed the Australian coast just south of Adelaide. I played tag with my itch for the entire three minutes we took to cross over New South Wales to the east coast just south of Brisbane. That left us about twenty minutes of South Pacific Islands and open ocean before we commenced our drop. Things seemed to be going pretty well. Snug in my *Gryphon* cacoon, I was feeling more confident with each passing island, each Pacific squall, and each wide open patch of Pacific blue.

※

By the time we were five minutes out—that's 2,500 klicks—I began to feel a bit of…I wouldn't call it anxiety…more like intense anticipation. I wanted to get the show on the road, itch or no itch.

"Standby," Mother said at the one-minute mark.

Based on her precise calculations, Mother actually commenced the retro-burn about ten seconds earlier than our plan called for, but I was confident. She knew what she was doing. Two minutes or so later—you'll have to examine the log to get the exact number—Mother cut the kick thruster burn and rotated the pallets back, so we were pointed in our direction of travel.

"Good luck and Godspeed!" Master Chief Boldt said as I felt the jolt of pallet separation and on my heads-up watched six expended pallets drop away to burn up in the atmosphere.

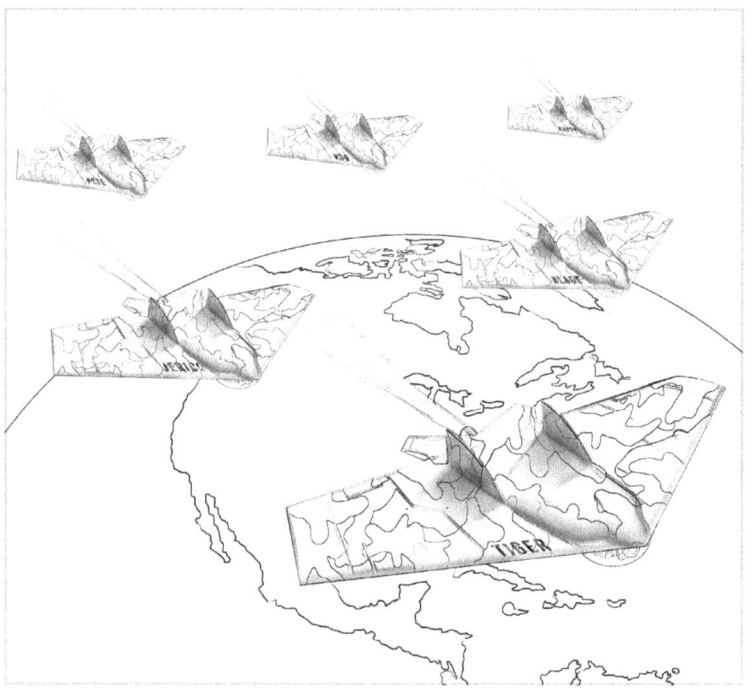

Figure 16—Tiger Baily's SWIC team in formation in LEO preparing to drop.

"Forward velocity six-eight-hundred meters-per-second," Mother told me. I knew she was also talking to the rest of my squad, and I trusted that she was doing whatever was necessary to keep us in formation. On my heads-up, I saw the individual *Gryphons* increasing their separation until we each were a hundred meters distant from the closest *Gryphon*.

We were accelerating toward the ocean at 9.8 m/sec² while heading toward the horizon at 6,800 m/sec. Mother had set a timer when she separated my pallet. Drop timer digits flashed at the right side of my display. At the three-minute mark, the California coast was fifty klicks below, and ten seconds later, we began to grab atmosphere. As things started to heat up, I checked our formation. We still held position. "Report!" I ordered.

"Rog warmin' up!"

"Slade toasty!"

"Jerico friggin' hot, Boss!"

"Cappy ditto!"

"Pete too!"

"Take us up, Mother," I said. Okay thus far. I was feeling pretty good about it.

Mother had already set our nozzles and wing torques to optimize our return to space. I felt weight return and then disappear as Mother cut the burn and announced, "Forward velocity five-zero-eight meters-per-second, net forward transfer nine-three-zero kilometers."

Given what we were doing, that was about as close to being on the button as possible.

Mother reset the timer as our vertical motion slowed to zero, and then together we plunged back into the atmosphere, slowing down to about Mach 14 and eating up another 700 klicks before it got too hot to continue. By the time we dove into our third dip, we were down to Mach 5, and the guys were letting go *Hooyahs* as we whipped back out for the last time.

"Stay focused!" I ordered. I really didn't want something to go wrong this far into the exercise.

The next drop put us at thirty-five klicks above and 150 klicks west of our drop zone at sixty m/sec. It took us a few minutes to work our way down to 8,000 meters above Death Valley. Our destination lay about 50 klicks due east in the Amargosa Valley

We had made it. All that remained was landing and hitching a ride to Vegas. And that's when all hell broke loose!

DEATH VALLEY—BIRD STRIKE

"What the fuck was that?" Jerico yelled, his Hispanic twang quite evident. Then I heard a loud crunch as my heads-up display went crazy.

"Shit!" I yelped as my *Gryphon* commenced rolling hard to the right. Mother automatically torqued my wings to compensate but without much success. I activated my hypergolic rocket, but nothing happened.

I cleared the alarms in my heads-up display and moved them to the right corner. I could see my squad in formation behind me as I lost altitude on a rolling plunge from 8,000 meters. Chief Slade's blip moved above my position.

"You got a hole the size of Cappy's head in your right wing," he said. "You ain't got no UDMH left."

"Tell me about it," I muttered.

"I got a problem here, Control," I said, trying to keep my voice steady. I briefly described my situation. "I will need some immediate help to get out of this."

❋

"I gotcha, Tiger," Jerico said as he maneuvered alongside me, matched my roll, and slipped his left wing under my damaged right. This was something we had never practiced, but Jerico was the best flyer in SWIC, next to me, of course. He stopped my roll and stabilized my wingsuit. I could almost feel stability flowing from his wing to mine.

"Mother, work both units as one," I ordered. And to Jerico, "Think we can make Amargosa Valley?"

"We ain't goin' nowhere but down, Boss," Jerico said to me. "Ain't never been to Death Valley."

As we flew together, I could feel his wing varying pressure against mine as surrounding air currents buffeted our ungainly marriage.

"Rog," I ordered, "take command and complete the mission. Set down in Amargosa Valley as planned. Jerico and I are taking a detour."

DEATH VALLEY SNAG

The *Gryphon-10* has a glide ratio of 14 to 1, meaning that for every meter we dropped, we moved fourteen forward. My *Gryphon* and Jerico's flying together didn't come close to that.

"What's our glide ratio, Mother," I asked.

"Five to one," she answered.

I glanced at my altitude gauge. It read 7,000 meters. That gave us a thirty-five klick range. My stomach dropped, and my itch returned.

"High mountains to the east and really high mountains to the west," I said to Jerico. "We can't make it over the eastern range. We gotta land in Death Valley. It's gonna be a hard landing, but you can pull up at the last moment with your rocket and come in easy. We really got no choice."

Jerico grunted a non-response. He was working pretty hard, keeping his wing in contact with mine.

"This is Control," Master Chief Boldt said. "Actually, you do…have a choice, I mean. I got an Air Force C-130 Herc ten minutes out. He's gonna set up so you can fly right into his cargo bay."

"Beats crash landing in Death Valley," I said.

"Hooyah!" Jerico muttered quietly.

Figure 17—C-130 Hercules aircraft receiving Tiger Baily's damaged Gryphon with assistance from Jerico.

Eight minutes later, the lumbering aircraft hove into view, pulled in front of us, and matched our speed and drop rate.

"Tiger, this is Randy Dorsey. Here's what we're gonna do." In just a few seconds, he laid out the plan for us.

"You ready to do this, Jerico?" I asked.

"Hooyah!" he said.

"I'm slowing, Tiger," Dorsey said as he lowered his cargo ramp.

We began to drift toward the open maw of the Herc. It looked pretty small from where we were.

"Slowing more," Dorsey said. We drifted closer—fifty meters out.

"Ten-knot difference between us," Dorsey said.

Twenty-five meters…

"Eight-knot difference…"

Twenty meters…I checked my altitude. Only 2,000 meters. We were below the mountain peaks on either side of us.

"Five-knot difference…"

Five meters out…

"Three-knot difference…"

We were over the ramp, Mother maneuvering us by torquing my left and Jerico's right wings. Suddenly, the big aircraft dropped three meters. One moment we were ready to set down on the ramp, the next, the Herc was falling away below us. We got separated by the turbulence from this lumbering beast, and I did a complete rollover before Jerico synched to my movement and slipped his left wing back under my right.

"Thanks, Jerico, that feels good!"

"Hooyah!" Jerico grunted as he fought to keep us together. Mother dropped us back and down to the Herc's level. Fleeting images of Apryl whipped across my mind as we struggled to hold the *Gryphons* together.

"Let's give it another go, Randy," I said, forcing my voice to remain calm like the cool fighter pilots in holovision broadcasts.

"Roger that, Tiger. Ready to try again. The road is a bit bumpy, so stay alert!"

Once more, we aimed at the cargo opening, Mother keeping us to the right.

"Back off!" Randy ordered as the Herc bounced up about a meter. Apparently, Mother saw it coming because she dropped us back and away from the ramp.

"Okay," Randy said, "bring her in now!"

With some remaining forward motion and the ramp just a meter below us, we reached the forward-right edge of the ramp. My right wing and all of Jerico extended off the ramp's right side. Jerico dropped and pulled away as my lower carapace and both wings hit the ramp. My forward motion caused my right-wing to strike the cargo hatch edge, spinning me clockwise into the hold.

As Jerico dropped his nose, he said, "I can't make it to Amargosa, and I ain't gonna land in no fricken Death Valley." He did a full 360 on his rocket, flew toward the ramp, and slid into the C-130 cargo hold, retracting his wings as he did so.

"Nice flyin'," Dorsey said as he closed the ramp.

DAEDALUS SQUAD—FINALE

Rog and the rest of the squad landed without incident in Amargosa Valley, a stone's throw from some kind of a mechanized dairy farm. We met the next day in Vegas, where we celebrated as only sailors can.

Oh yeah, about what happened over Death Valley…You may not believe this, but we ran into a flock of migrating geese, at 8,000 meters no less. Who tracks migrating geese? Especially at 8,000 meters? They've been seen before at this altitude, but it's rare. Their presence over Death Valley at our arrival was a complete fluke. They were doing 10 kph; we were doing about 200. They lost one of theirs, and we almost lost me. I guess we both were lucky.

This time we actually managed to keep our exploit secret. The Commander-in-Chief was delighted with the proof of concept outcome and invited us to visit him in the Oval Office. Drinking a fine scotch with The

Boss in that room was something else. We discussed several interesting things, but I can't tell you about that.

We proved we could do it. We've done it several times since. Now we're fully ready for a combat drop. I'll let you know when that finally happens.

DAEDALUS COMBAT
SWIC Combat Drop from Low Earth Orbit

Chapter Four

CHAPTER FOUR

DAEDALUS COMBAT

MOZAMBIQUE CHANNEL—200 KILOMETERS NORTHEAST OF MAYOTTE ISLAND

The explosion showered Capt. Mansur Darusman with thousands of tempered glass shards as the windscreens on the bridge of the Tasmanian Cruise Ship *CS Platypus* burst inward. Darusman slammed to the deck bleeding from dozens of cuts on face and hands, the front of his captain's uniform shredded. As he painfully raised himself to one knee, his undamaged eyes, shielded by cracked but still intact glasses, sought the source of the explosion. In good weather, he kept the weathertight doors to the flying bridges latched but not sealed. The explosion had blown both open. He got to his feet and turned to his right.

A dark-skinned man wearing a white turban-like headcloth, blue tee-shirt and khaki trousers, shod in ragged sneakers, and carrying an AK-47, stepped through the door and fired a burst of three shots, striking the captain's right arm and shoulder. Darusman dropped back to the deck as the pirate swept the bridge with his fire, killing everyone but the captain.

"Senator…senator!" the Pirate screamed, pointing his weapon at Darusman's head.

Darusman got to his feet slowly, left hand in the air, right dangling uselessly at his side.

Another pirate entered the left bridge door and pointed his weapon at the captain. He also wore a headcloth, but his tee-shirt was pink with black trousers. His sneakers were even more ragged than the first pirate's.

The first pirate waved the other one down and screamed again, "Senator! Senator!" Then he commenced pushing and prodding the captain toward a door at the back of the bridge.

"No! No!" Darusman said, trying not to sound challenging. He reached for the mike to the general announcing system and held it up in his open hand.

Both pirates pointed their weapons at his head.

"The Senator," Darusman said, waving the mike. "Senator Manfred…"

The first pirate nodded with a grin displaying several missing teeth.

Darusman pressed the General Announcing call button with his thumb, "Senator Manfred, Senator Jack Manfred, your presence is requested on the bridge. Senator Manfred, please come to the bridge." Then he surreptitiously pressed a second button on the mike. "Mayday, Mayday…Tasmanian *CS Platypus* hijacked…Mayday… Mayd…"

Both pirates fired, splattering Capt. Darusman's brains all over the bridge.

※

A young airman in AFRICOM Mozambique headquarters intercepted a Mayday message and passed it to his supervising sergeant.

A Navy Radioman in Diego Garcia intercepted a Mayday call and passed it to his Chief-of-the-Watch.

A Radioman on a U.S. Navy cruiser patrolling the Gulf of Aden picked up a distress call and passed it to his Officer-of-the-Deck.

Within fifteen minutes, a tanker aircraft was dispatched from AFRICOM Mozambique, two Navy jet fighters were scrambled from a U.S. Carrier on patrol near the Gulf of Oman, and SWIC-3 was mobilized at its newly established base on Howland Island in the equatorial Pacific.

Ten minutes after this, Lt.Col. Randal Dorsey was located on leave in Germany on a Rhein River cruise. He was picked up by helicopter from the river cruise ship, whisked to Ramstein Air Base, and from thence to a supersonic executive jet belonging to Ramstein's commanding general.

Two-and-a-half-hours later, Dorsey stepped onto the tarmac at Antsiranana International Airport on the northern tip of Madagascar…just as SWIC-3 skipper Lt.Cdr. Derek "Tiger" Baily, with paramedic Apryl Searson and the senior five members of Squad One, arrived at Amelia Earhart Skyport eighty kilometers above Baker Island.

AMELIA EARHART SKYPORT—PRELAUNCH

I pulled myself away from Apryl and jumped out of bed to get dressed as I took an audio call from SWIC Commanding Officer Navy Capt. Brad Nelson. SWIC-3 was being mobilized, he said, and we had to get to Amelia Earhart Skyport as quickly as possible.

"I'll get the Team moving, Brad, and call you back," I told him.

I put a Link override call to Lt. Roger Brook. "Mobilize the Team," I told him. "You, Slade, Jerico, Cappy, and Pete will fly with me. Assemble a support team and meet me topside."

I called Nelson back. "Okay," I said, "we'll be ready to launch in thirty minutes or less."

"Here's the situation," Brad said. "Senator Jack Manfred…"

"The one who's likely to be the next President?" I asked, interrupting.

"The same," Brad said. "He, his wife, and daughter are on vacation in the Indian Ocean on the Tasmanian cruise ship *CS Platypus*—or I should say, *were*. *Platypus* has been hijacked in the waters north of Madagascar. We don't know much yet, but the French government tells us that pirates are operating out of Mayotte Island."

"Mayotte Island?" I had no idea where or what it was.

"Used to be a French Insular Department, like Hawaii to us, but a decade ago rebels overran the island, and France decided it was not worth recovering. Mayotte has been sustaining itself through small-time piracy."

"Looks like they graduated to the big time," I said.

"That's one way of putting it," Nelson quipped. "Your job is to rescue Senator Manfred and get the ship back."

"Lethal force?" I asked.

"Authorized," Nelson answered.

I headed out the door with Apryl in my wake.

"A couple of Navy fighters will locate *Platypus*," Nelson told me. "Dorsey will arrive at Antsiranana on the northern tip of Madagascar by the time you launch. We got him because of his previous aerial pickup experience. The Madagascar Air Force has agreed to let him fly one of their C-130s.

"We assume the pirates are taking the *Platypus* to Mayotte. It has the largest lagoon of any island. We expect them to dock at the Port of Longoni on the northern side of Mayotte. We're redirecting a surveillance satellite to get you the best possible intel. By the time you are ready to drop, we will have uploaded all the details into Mother."

Apryl and I climbed aboard a waiting Chinook and departed for Baker. We kept the *Gryphons* in ready storage on Baker to enable more rapid deployment. The Team landed at Baker a few minutes following my alert and had checked out each wingsuit by the time we arrived. Both Rog and Slade had checked my unit out, so I held off checking it myself until our arrival at the skyport.

Our capsule arrived at Amelia Earhart Skyport, tilted to horizontal, and sealed against the skyport lock. After the door opened inward, Apryl and I stepped into the reception area to join my guys.

"Everyone okay physically?" I asked.

"I got a bit of an earache," Jerico said.

Slade glowered at him, but Apryl walked over to him and inserted her otoscope into his left ear. Then she pulled it out and kissed his ear. "Is that better?" she asked to the howls of the other guys.

"I think my right ear's hurting now," Jerico said, but shut up when Slade slapped the back of his head.

※

"This is for real, guys," I said as they formed up loosely in front of me. I told them about the *Platypus*, the pirates, the Senator, the Senator's family, and Dorsey. "Here's how we'll do it," I said. "Jerico and I will head inland on

Mayotte Island to coordinates Mother will receive just before we drop and maybe even during our drop. The four of you," I indicated the others, "will take the ship, take out the pirates, and get the hell out of Dodge."

I pulled up a holoimage Nelson had sent me. "We think they will tie the ship up here." I pointed to the Longoni Container Ship Dock. "We're dropping in late night. Pete—you hit the dock and cut the mooring hawsers. Rog and Slade, you take the bridge and get the ship underway. Cappy, you take out the rest of the bad guys…lethal force is authorized—take no prisoners!"

"Hooyah!" Chief Slade said, joined by the rest. "Hooyah!"

"Pete, as soon as you can safely do so, get airborne and join Rog and the others." I stopped to let the instructions sink in. "We know they got small arms. Don't know about shoulder-launched missiles. You know that we added rear-facing energy-beam weapons to each *Mark five Gryphon*. Mother should be able to take out anything fired at your rear." I stopped and looked each guy in his eyes. "Rog, you and Slade gonna have to get the *Platypus* from Mayotte to Antsiranana on Madagascar. We'll send you a pilot to dock it, and will try to get him on board sooner if possible." I looked around. "Any questions?" I asked.

"Can Apryl check my right ear?" Jerico asked with a plaintive tone.

"Knock it off, Jerico!" Slade said to a *Hooyah!* from the full Team.

AMELIA EARHART SKYPORT—LAUNCH

We had gone through this exercise so often that the process had nearly become routine. Backed up by Senior Chief Bob Baxter, I kept a watchful eye on the guys to make sure that routine didn't cause them to miss something.

While the guys suited up, I descended to the lower level with Apryl. We gazed together through the large downward looking window. The sky-tower disappeared in the haze below us. Isolated swirling cloud formations filled the sky to the horizon in all directions. A storm was coming. Apryl wrapped her arms around my neck and kissed me softly.

"You come back to me, Sailor…you hear me?" She was near tears.

I held her close and whispered, "It's okay, Apryl. Nothing's going to happen."

"You don't know that," she said through tears that were now rolling down her cheeks. "It isn't just Mother Nature now. There's bad guys at the other end."

I kissed her tears away. "I know," I said softly. "I'll be careful, I promise."

She looked up at me, her blue eyes overflowing. "You better," she said and ran up the stairs.

✺

In a matter of minutes, the *Gryphon* team was suited up, including weapon battery backs, and both Rog and Slade were on their way down the rail, followed in short order by Jerico, Cappy, and Pete, while I was giving my *Gryphon* a final detailed check. The guys strapped me in and lowered my carapace cover. As the gantry hoisted me, I pushed Apryl's ministrations to the back of my mind and concentrated on the task at hand, which at the moment was the returning itch on my right buttock—obviously a psychological manifestation that accompanied my launches.

As I accelerated down the rail, picking up velocity for 1,300 klicks, I told myself, *Here you go again on a "we've never done this before" mission, and this time bad guys with weapons are waiting for us when we get there.*

SLINGSHOT RAIL

Routine is routine, even if it is not precisely the same. Exactly four minutes and ten seconds after launch, Mother rotated my pallet 30° to the left. Thirty-two seconds later and 1,327 klicks down the rail, Mother released my pallet and initiated a two-minute-ten-second kick thruster burn. We headed away from the Earth at almost 8 km/s on a Hohmann Transfer Orbit (HTO) that passed 240 klicks to the north and 19 klicks above Fred Noonan Skyport, not that different from my first Squad drop. Apogee was over Lagos, Nigeria, as before, where I expected to meet the other five team members.

I relaxed into freefall and allowed myself to think about Apryl for a few minutes while we flew over the eastern Pacific and Mexico. As we approached the Atlantic south of Florida and the nighttime terminator, I began to give serious thought to exactly how we would carry out our mission once we descended through the nighttime sky over the Indian Ocean north of Madagascar.

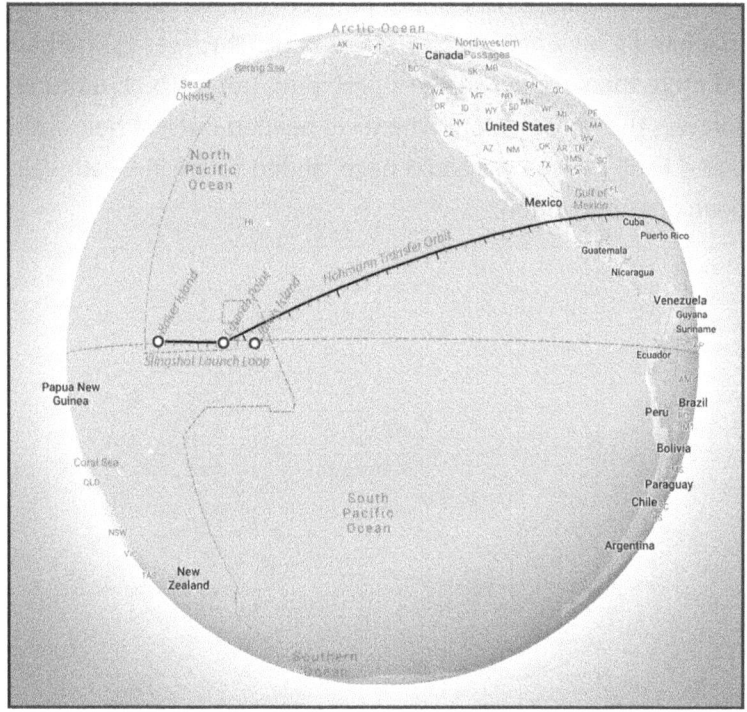

Figure 18—Slingshot Space Launch Loop with the Hohmann Transfer Orbit.

LEO

Unlike our first Squad drop, where we traveled half-way around the world after our circularizing burn so that we could drop into southern Nevada, this time, we would commence our drop seven minutes after we attained LEO. We would be over western Tanzania, just east of Lake

Rukwa. At least, that was the plan Capt. Nelson and the Coronado team put together.

Mother was very good at bringing us together at apogee. I used to hover over her shoulder to make sure she got it right, but lately, I discovered I had better things to do. As I climbed higher along my HTO, while playing tag with my itch, I didn't bother with the grand view of the Earth below. I was too preoccupied with thinking up contingencies after the drop and finding their solutions. During our many orbital drops, we really had gotten a handle on what Mother Nature could throw at us. We had experienced more than our fair share of problems, but my high-altitude goose collision was the only incident where we needed outside help—although Jerico and I still believe we could have landed safely in Death Valley had that been our only option.

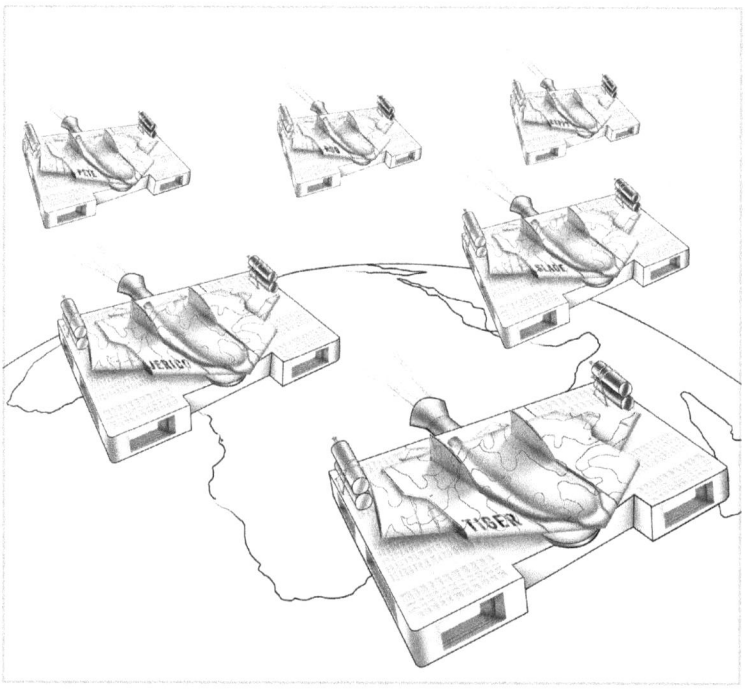

Figure 19—Tiger Baily's SWIC team in LEO preparing for drop.

Lagos was a brilliant jewel blazing in the darkened landscape 160 klicks below me. I pulled into position at the formation point right after Mother accomplished my circularizing burn.

"Hey, guys," I said. "Extinguish your nav lights, and let's do this!"

Five *Hooyahs!* sounding as one filled my helmet. We were ready to go.

LEO—COMBAT DROP

As soon as I got into position at the tip of the formation, I ordered Mother to reverse our pallets in preparation for deorbiting. While Mother rotated the pallets with our gyros, I followed the process on my heads-up. I know I've said it before, but the display was as close to a video game as you can get—especially here in LEO.

"We drop in four minutes," I said. "Everybody good?" I was concerned because this was the first time that anybody had dropped from LEO into a combat scenario. My guys were Navy SEALS. There was no combat situation they couldn't handle, but this was so dramatically different from anything any warrior had ever done before, that I wanted assurance that my team members had no second thoughts.

I got five ragged *Hooyahs!* back—what else could I have expected?—and then Mother initiated the deorbiting burn.

Mother cut our burn, rotated each of us so we were once again pointed in our direction of travel, and then she dropped our pallets. I felt a slight tug as my automatic, self-sealing oxygen connector broke away. About thirty seconds later, I watched five bright flashes from five pallets with their oxygen and hypergolic fuel tanks burning up in the nighttime atmosphere. I did not spot the sixth one before they plunged into the cloud layer.

Lake Rukwe lay about a hundred klicks off to our right, but it was too dark below us to see anything at all. A few minutes ahead on the coast was Mtwara. I vaguely remembered something about a failed groundnut export operation that was the reason for anything at all at this location. I don't think there's much there now. We were pretty busy skipping into and

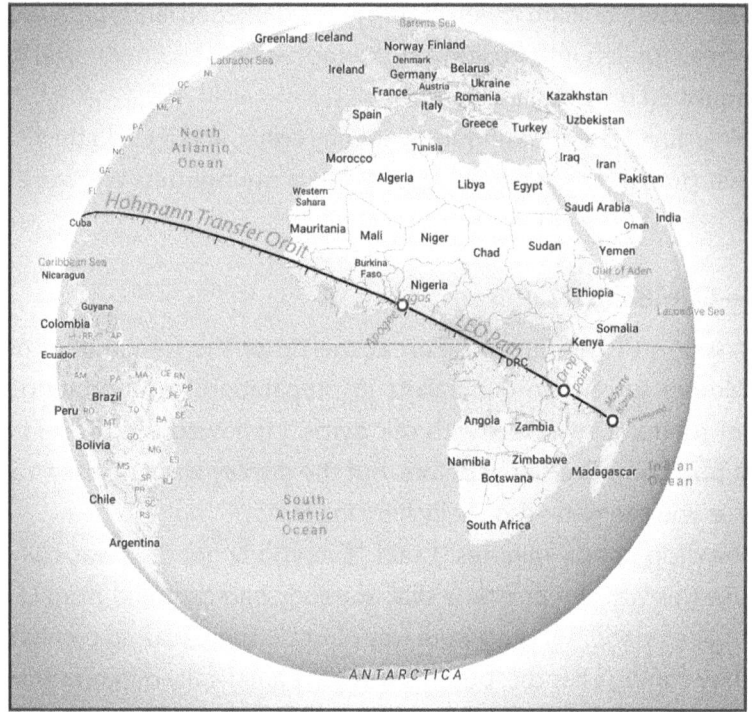

Figure 20—The Hohmann Transfer Orbit and the apogee with the shortened LEO path. The drop point and destination, Mayotte Island.

out of the atmosphere at that point, and I don't really remember if I saw any lights on the ground or not.

Besides, cloud cover obscured the surface every time we dipped down. Can you imagine what it's like at night, high over clouds, or dark jungle, or ocean? Nothing... black... nada... Thank goodness Mother knew where we were.

We broke out of our last dip at 8,000 meters. Mother said we were over Mayotte Island, but you could've fooled me. Above, the heavens were as bright as they ever were, but below lay a thick, turbulent storm system.

"Winds at five-thousand meters average fifty kph with gusts to ninety kph," Mother told us. "Heavy rain from 500 meters."

Control dropped the Mayotte Island layout onto my heads-up, pinpointing *Platypus* docked at the north Longoni pier and briefed me on the fighter cover.

"Squad, this is Tiger. *Platypus* has just docked at the north Longoni pier, port side to. Pete, you cut the lines. Rog, push away with your bow and stern thrusters, and then pull out with a hard-right-rudder. Pull around the point to the right into the middle of the lagoon. Navy fighters overhead will keep the bad guys away from the ship."

After I completed my instructions to the squad, Control continued briefing me. "Tiger, the senator's family is still aboard *Platypus*. Senator Manfred has been relocated to a small reservoir about seven-and-a-half klicks in the hills southeast of Port Longoni. Mother will get you there. You will need to locate him, terminate his guards, and get to the clear extraction point on the hill to the northwest. We'll drop you a Fulton surface-to-air recovery system for the senator and two bladders of pressurized hypergolic fuel to get you and Jerico to your airborne extraction point."

Almost as an afterthought, Control added, "The pirates have made a one-hundred-million-dollar demand for the senator's safe return."

※

"Listen up, everyone, this is Tiger," I said. "Drop down to a thousand meters. Watch the wind!"

"Tiger, this is Control. We just established contact with a *Platypus* crew member sequestered in the ship's forward chain locker. We described your wingsuits. He says you can land on each bridge wing and on the main deck just aft of the bow. He says the pirates are technically ignorant. A crew member had to sail and dock the ship for them. They have four men on board, one at the brow leading down to the dock, one in the Bridge, and two roaming guards. There's a fifth pirate roaming the dock."

"This is Tiger," I said. "Rog, make your assignments."

"This is Rog. Slade, take the starboard bridge wing—on your left as we fly in. Take out any bad guys in the bridge. I'll take the port and eliminate the brow guard. Cappy, land on the bow main deck, find those roaming guards and take them out. Pete, land on the dock near the bow. Take out the roving patrol, slice the mooring hawsers with your weapon, and get airborne ASAP. Any questions?"

He got three *Hooyahs!*

At a thousand meters, the wind was still a factor, but it seemed to be a steady blow from the ocean to the northeast, carrying a lot of rain. That was good for us—made us more difficult to spot, while we had Mother and our heads-up displays to guide us.

Rog and his guys dropped to 300 meters, setting up for the attack.

"On my six, Jerico!" I ordered as I vectored southeast and increased my descent rate as much as possible. Mother superimposed the terrain on my heads-up. The reservoir lay six klicks ahead, and beside it, between reservoir and extraction point, Senator Manfred's Link beacon flashed on my display.

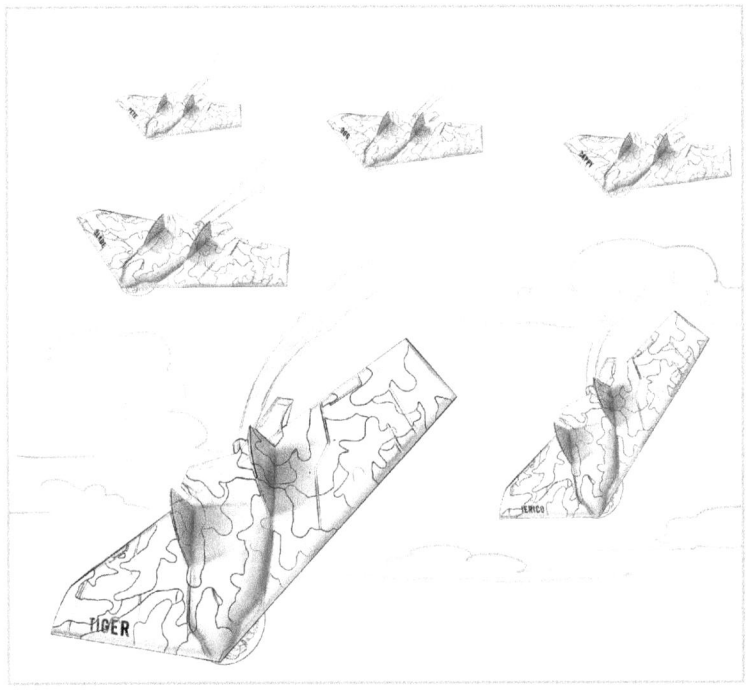

Figure 21—Rog and his team head to free CS Platypus. Tiger and Jerico on their way to rescue Senator Manfred.

MAYOTTE ISLAND—*CS PLATYPUS*

While Jerico and I were occupied inland, Rog and his team dropped straight down through the rain to one hundred meters above the calm lagoon waters. They flew over the *Platypus*, dropped to fifty meters, and made a bow-on approach. The dock was brilliantly lit. Pete dropped stealthily to the bright dock, grabbed his silent energy pulse weapon as he left his *Gryphon*, and took out the three nearest lights and the roving guard who was half-way between the bow and brow, walking away from Pete. The guard never knew what hit him. Rog landed on the port bridge wing, stepped out of his *Gryphon* with his weapon, and silently took out the guard at the brow three decks below him, and then he took out the two nearest dock lights. Simultaneously, Slade dropped to the starboard bridge wing, shed his *Gryphon*, and took out the unsuspecting bridge guard who had just turned to see what was happening on the port bridge wing. While this was happening, Pete ran along the dock burning through each hawser with a quick weapon burst. When he reached the last mooring, a bullet whizzed past his head. He turned, shot the pirate who had appeared on the road at the middle of the dock, and then he shot out the remaining dock light.

The prevailing wind had already pushed the *Platypus* away from the dock. Rog started the stern thruster and revved the main engines to full power. He threw the rudder hard right and willed the stern not to hit the dock.

Rog picked up the general announcing mike and said, "This is Lt. Roger Brook, U.S. Navy SEALS Winged Insertion Command. We have taken over this ship and eliminated most of the pirates. We are getting underway for Antsiranana, Madagascar. Please remain in your staterooms with your doors locked until I give you an *All Clear*."

Pete ran back toward his *Gryphon*, dodging several bullets as he ran. He returned fire at two of the flashpoints, without knowing if he got the shooters or not, and then he mounted his wingsuit and rocketed up into the driving rain.

Mother outlined *Platypus* in Pete's heads-up and then announced, "Incoming!" Before Pete had a chance to react, his rear-facing pulse weapon destroyed the incoming shoulder-fired missile. Pete raced over the north end of Longoni harbor to meet *Platypus* a kilometer into the broad lagoon. He came around to her bow, intending to land where Cappy had touched down earlier.

Still fifty meters out, as he dropped lower to land, a bright flash from below the bridge at the rear of the deck announced another missile launch. Before Pete had time to react, Mother aimed and fired his forward weapon, destroying the missile just three meters before impact. Cappy came out of the shadows and fired at the launch point of the missile. A pirate with a smoking hole in his chest fell forward out of the shadow.

Still twenty meters from the bow, Pete's rocket coughed and stopped, out of fuel. He set his wings for maximum glide, lifted his nose, and missing the bow by centimeters, landed softly on the darkened deck.

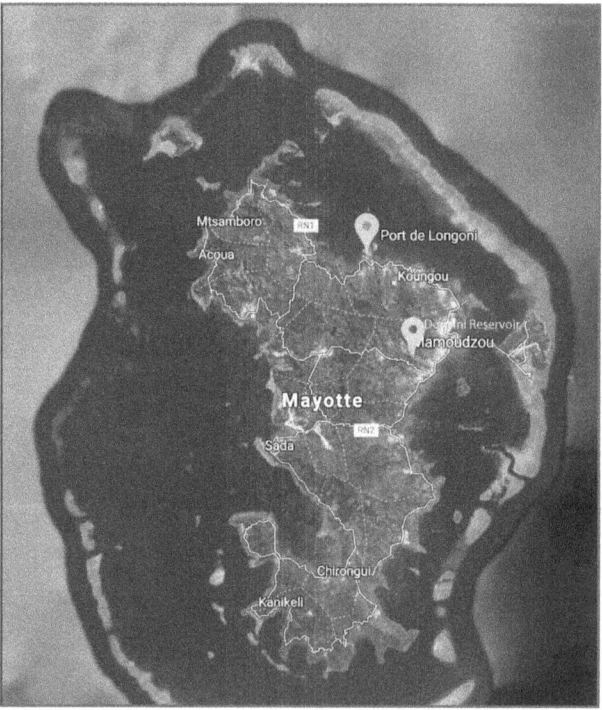

Figure 22—Mayotte Island with Port of Longoni and Doujani Reservoir

Suddenly, a shot rang out from the starboard side of the ship, hitting Cappy's right shoulder, spinning him around as he fell. Pete rolled out of his *Gryphon* while drawing his weapon and fired at the flashpoint just as Slade on the bridge wing above did the same. A loud scream filled the darkness as the last pirate stumbled out onto the main forward deck, left arm completely missing and his right shoulder mangled beyond recognition. When he saw the two SEALS, he shook his head in total disbelief and threw himself over the rail into the dark lagoon waters.

MAYOTTE ISLAND—DOUJANI RESERVOIR

It took about twenty minutes to get to Doujani Reservoir, using most of our remaining fuel. We landed silently in a narrow clearing about 250 meters to the northwest of and fifty meters above the reservoir. We exited the *Gryphons*, holstered our weapons, and discarded our helmets. My Link showed that Senator Manfred was down the slope in a clump of trees about twenty meters from the water's edge.

Wearing night-vision glasses, and getting soaked by the rain, Jerico and I crept to the edge of the slope. Mother was hooked into our Links. She superimposed the senator's exact position over our night vision view. I activated my infra-red sensor. Down by the water, four heat sources clumped together, and another was a couple of meters to the side. I slowly scanned a full circle around me. Other than a couple of obvious night critters, I saw nothing else.

I placed a finger to my lips and signaled Jerico to circle around to the left. I indicated I would circle right. I pointed to him, held up two fingers, and then slashed across my throat. I pointed at myself and indicated the same. He nodded.

I crept down the slope to my right, any sound I made muffled by the rain. Although I couldn't see Jerico, I knew he was doing the same to the left. We both reached the clump of trees with the Pirates and Manfred about five minutes later. We drew our weapons and aimed. Four energy bolts silently removed the heads of the hapless pirates. Senator Manfred's eyes got big as platters, but to his credit, he didn't utter a sound.

I stepped in front of the senator and whispered quietly, "Navy SEALS. Are there any other bad guys?"

He swallowed and shook his head, his eyes large with fright. I saw him make a conscious effort to quell his shaking hands. I gestured him to follow us. He did so silently, clearly aware of what was at stake. When we got to the clearing, I signaled Control.

"We have the senator. Ready to receive the Fulton system."

"Tiger, this is Randy Dorsey. I'm in a Herc a thousand meters overhead with several members of your SWIC team—Benny, Piggy, and Cowboy—and a Fulton ready for a guided paradrop. I see your marker, but we are dealing with significant winds aloft. Your guys will remotely guide the Fulton down to the two-hundred-meter level. Then you take over. It has IR markers so you can see it with your night vision."

"I got it, Randy. Let her fly!"

Mother gave me a clear view in my glasses. The Fulton kept drifting to the west, but my SWIC team members in the Herc kept pulling it back overhead. At 200 meters, I took over, and as it got lower, the winds lessened. At seventy-five meters, I started to make out the four IR beacons, one at each corner. I eased the Fulton in and set it down just two meters from where we crouched.

I glanced over at the Senator. He seemed to have gotten his emotions under control. I knew from news reports that he was a man used to being in control. This had to be entirely outside his experience. "How are you holding up, Senator?" I asked.

He responded with a slight grin and shrugged shoulders. "This is way outside my MOS," he said quietly.

I lifted my eyebrows at his response. "Army Ranger," he said and gave me his old unit.

"Hooyah!" I responded as we exchanged high-fives.

"Any news on my family?" he asked.

"My guys took the ship," I told him. "they should be safe."

Jerico removed the fuel bladders from the pallet, and then set up the Fulton while I explained the next steps to the senator. Jerico handed him a harness. I showed him how to put it on.

"Jerico is inflating a helium balloon with a strong bungee line attached. We will attach the bungee line to your harness, and then you will stand facing that way." I pointed into the wind. "Jerico will let the balloon rise to two-hundred meters. Randy will fly a line of position in his C-130 at near stall speed toward the balloon and will snag the line with a yoke installed on his nose. You will go flying into the air where crew members will hook your line, and you will be reeled into the cargo hatch." I grinned at him. "It's like a super exciting amusement park ride."

He looked at me with a bit of a lopsided grin. "I've done a lot of things," he said, "but this will be a first." We exchanged another high-five.

We walked to where Jerico had rigged the blimp-shaped balloon.

"It's on its way to two hundred meters," Jerico said. "Let's get you hooked up." He securely attached the senator's harness to the bungee cord with two stainless carabiners. "You ready?" Jerico asked.

"I am." I could see his jaw set tightly.

"Gimme five!" Jerico held up his gloved hand.

DOUJANI RESERVOIR SNAG

I notified Dorsey that we were ready.

"Expect me in ten or less," Dorsey answered.

Seven minutes later, Senator Jack Manfred, former Army Ranger, ex-hostage, probable future U.S. President, whisked silently into the dark, rainy sky.

While we were waiting, Jerico had fueled our *Gryphons*. We donned our helmets, climbed into our wingsuits, and rocketed into the wet darkness.

"We're airborne, Randy. How's your passenger?"

"He's on board, none the worse for wear, and he expresses his thanks. Oh…and he talked with his wife. His family's safe."

"Tell him he can thank us in person in a few minutes," I said. "You got us on radar."

"'Sa fact," Dorsey said. "I'm doin' one-hundred-fifty, three hundred meters ahead of you."

Figure 23—The Fulton ground-to-air extraction system

"We're coming tandem," I said. "Jerico first. I'll be ten meters behind and ten below."

The open maw of the C-130 appeared out of the darkness in front of and a couple meters below us, its cargo bay brilliantly lit. Jerico dropped onto the ramp, cut his rocket, retracted his wings, and with one smooth move slid into the cargo bay. Dorsey dropped the Herc ten meters, and I set up to duplicate Jerico's maneuver.

At that moment, Mother interrupted with "Incoming!" She dropped my *Gryphon* several meters while simultaneously firing several bursts at the incoming missile from my rear weapon. The first two missed, but the third one struck the missile's rocket engine just a meter behind *my* nozzle. The missile disintegrated without exploding and fell back to earth.

"Okay, Tiger, let's try again," Dorsey said in his calm aviator's voice.

As I brought my *Gryphon* around to get into position, Mother again announced, "Incoming!" She launched a volley at the missile, but before they affected it, the missile broke up in mid-air as it was struck by hundreds of rapid-fire .50 cal. bullets. Immediately thereafter, a large explosion enveloped the entire clearing that we had so recently vacated.

"That should simplify things," a new voice said on the circuit. "Lt. Joe 'Happy' Snider, U.S. Navy, at your service."

"Thanks, Happy, I owe you one. Tiger out!"

※

My *Gryphon* ceased sliding along the Herc deck, and I secured my electronics and popped open my clamshell. As I swung to vertical, to my utter astonishment, I found myself wrapped in a tangle of female arms and legs.

"Tiger, Tiger…You're safe! You're safe!"

My helmet disappeared, and I experienced the most intense, tear-flooded liplock of my life. As I surfaced from its intensity, I began to hear laughter and cheering.

"Apryl…What the…How the hell did you get here?" I was genuinely mystified.

"She reached out to your command," Dorsey said, stepping into my view. "Somehow, they got her to Antsiranana in time to board my Herc—in her medical capacity, of course. She insisted that she knew you and your team medically better than anyone. Who was I to argue?"

MAYOTTE ISLAND—LAGOON

On board the *Platypus*, Pete did a quick field dressing on Cappy's shoulder. His spacesuit was shot, but that didn't matter. Cappy was alive and could function even though he was not a lefty.

On the bridge, Rog set his radar for close-in.

"Slade, watch the waters around us. We don't want a surprise boarding."

As they watched, twenty small craft departed Longoni Harbor, spotlights sweeping the water before them. "I'm getting underway," Rog said. "Get the others down on the main deck, ready to fire." He brought up the navigation system and pointed the cruise ship toward the nearest deep opening in the coral reef. Unlike a small craft, a large ship takes its time to build up speed, and Rog didn't want to move any faster than he thought he could handle through the slot in the reef.

As the watercraft closed the *Platypus*, the pirates commenced firing their small arms. "Hold fire until you are certain to be effective," Rog told his crew.

Suddenly, rapid-fire rained from above as two Navy fighters swept over the water between *Platypus* and the approaching small craft armada.

"This is Lt. Joe 'Happy' Snider and Lt. Bob 'Borax' Johnson, U.S. Navy, at your service! Tally Ho!"

Half the small craft floundered with the first pass. A second pass took out most of the remainder. As both fighters rose steeply into the night sky, a lone shoulder-fired missile chased them as they disappeared. The missile flamed out before it reached the clouds.

DAEDALUS COMBAT—FINALE

Rog turned out to be a pretty good ship handler. He successfully maneuvered *Platypus* out of Mayotte Lagoon and got underway for Antsiranana on Madagascar. The ship's doctor did a professional job on Cappy's shoulder. He was ready to party by the time *Platypus* reached port.

Jerico, Apryl, and I, along with Senator Manfred, arrived at Antsiranana International Airport a couple of hours after we successfully boarded Randy's Herc. Senator Manfred was whisked off by chopper to *Platypus* to see his family. The rest of the SWIC team refused to let us do anything. They serviced our *Gryphons* and wheedled out of us every detail of our pirate adventure. By the time we walked into the airport proper, the world media had arrived. We became the heroes of the hour and remained thus until Rog brought *Platypus* into the waters off Antsiranana. A pilot brought the ship to dock, and then the media forgot Jerico and me while they proceeded to court Rog and his guys—and rightly so. They were the ones who got shot up rescuing over 500 innocent passengers.

When the media learned that we had all dropped from LEO, except for Apryl, of course, who clung to me the entire time, the circus started all over again. It literally took us two days to extricate ourselves.

For a second time, we got to meet with the Commander-in-Chief. His personal friend and hand-picked successor, Senator Jack Manfred, was in the Oval Office with us. Rescuing him, saving his life, gave all of us special status with the Boss.

So, now the World knows about SWIC. It knows that Navy SEALS can appear absolutely anywhere at all, at any time. And that's a good thing.

PLEASE POST A REVIEW FOR THE DAEDALUS FILES

ON

AMAZON.COM AND GOODREADS.COM

I really appreciate you posting a review on Amazon and Goodreads. Posting to Amazon.com is intuitive. To post a review on Goodreads.com, click on this link, or go to their website and become a member if you are not already one. Search for *Daedalus*, and click on the "Want to read" button under the image of *Daedalus*. Indicate that you have read *Daedalus* and then you will be able to post a review. Thank you very much for going through this effort!

EXCERPT FROM THE FIRST CHAPTER OF: SLINGSHOT

by

Robert G. Williscroft

EQUATORIAL PACIFIC—SOUTHEAST OF BAKER ISLAND

Margo stopped kicking her feet as the ominous gray shapes flashed into her peripheral view. Long, tawny hair floated past her head as her feet dropped below her slim, brightly clad body. She took a deep breath and floated slightly upward. A hint of fear crept into her mind as she turned toward three gray, sleek predators cruising just inside the limit of her vision, about twenty-five meters away.

A gentle touch on her shoulder startled her. She turned to see Alex Regent tapping the depth reading on his dive-console with his index finger. Margo reached down and grasped her console, turning it so she could read her depth: twenty-five meters. She had drifted upward five meters since seeing the sharks.

Margo exhaled angrily and let some air out of her breathing bag. She knew better than to lose track of her depth. Out there, her life depended on a constant awareness of exactly how deep she was. Together she and Alex sank back to thirty meters. Off to their right, the three gray shapes drifted with them. Would she ever get used to it, she thought, as she released a bit of air into her bag to stop her descent.

"Alex," she said.

There was no response.

"Alex!" She tapped the back of her console several times.

"Alex!" Nothing but silence.

Alex placed himself in front of Margo and looked into her facemask. With his right hand, he formed a circle with thumb and forefinger. His three other fingers extended straight up.

Margo returned the sign indicating she was all right while nodding vigorously. Then she pointed to her ear and lifted her console, tapping the back. Alex fumbled at his ear, and then tapped his console, and then shook his head.

Great, Margo thought, *EFCom is busted just when we really need it. Not busted,* she corrected herself, *just a submerged antenna.* She pointed to the three menacing shapes off to her right. Alex turned and scanned around them. Above and just behind them, the blue-painted hull of their boat bobbed in the gentle waves. About twenty meters ahead of them hung a smooth, horizontal fluorescent orange tube about one meter in diameter. To the left, it stretched into the gloom; to the right, it angled downward. The fluorescent tube was attached to a slender cable angling up to the shadow of a buoy just beneath the surface to their right. Alex turned back toward Margo, making an exaggerated shrug.

Margo reached for her dive-console again and pressed a button located prominently on its face. The three sharks turned and commenced a meandering movement toward the two divers. Their front fins extended stiffly downward at about forty-five degrees. Their backs arched slightly, and their blunt snouts moved back and forth as they approached.

Margo felt her hair stand up on the nape of her neck. She turned to Alex and motioned him to her side. Alex withdrew a telescoped baton from its holder at his waist and extended it to its full one-and-a-half-meter length. He checked the safety lever near its handle, and with his thumb, he flicked the lever so it pointed forward. As the sharks drew nearer, he held the stick out in front of him, pointed in their direction. Margo glanced around them again and pushed her console button once more. Alex waved the stick about slowly and then steadied up on the nearest of the three menacing monsters.

Suddenly, with blurring speed, the nearest shark attacked. Alex struck out with his stick, the jolt of its impact rocking him backward. A sharp crack was followed by a hissing sound as carbon dioxide rushed into the shark's body. In the same moment, flashes of silvery-black streaked from several directions. One of the remaining sharks was struck broadside by a dolphin's blunt nose. In a flash, it disappeared.

The animal Alex had injected rolled on its side and began a crazed, uncontrolled spiral toward the surface thirty meters above them. On its way up, it was hit several times by charging dolphins. It expired of massive embolisms before reaching fifteen meters. In the melee, the third shark vanished.

Margo reached out for Alex, grabbed a handful of breathing bag, and pulled him close to her. She placed the flat of her full-facemask against his and looked deeply into his eyes, as close to a kiss as she could come under the circumstances. Even down here, they were deep blue. Several bubbles escaped from the positive pressure maintained inside their masks and shimmered their way toward the surface, expanding rapidly as they rose.

Like an old-time scuba diver, Margo thought, watching the rising silvery spheres. Instinctively she checked the volume in her breathing bag and glanced at the gauge on her tiny, ultra-high-pressure air flask. She found she was holding her breath, and as she felt the need to breathe, a gentle pressure developed against her back. She pulled back and turned to confront a two-and-a-half-meter-long dolphin nudging her from behind.

It was one of four that had responded to her sonic signal—George, her favorite. The other three dolphins crowded in around the neoprene and nylon suited divers, jostling each other for attention. Margo rubbed the head dome of each and indicated to Alex that he should do the same. Then the two of them turned their attention back to the tube suspended in front of them.

Alex swam to the angled portion and began to search along the tube's length, descending slowly. Margo dropped her arm from George's neck and kicked in Alex's direction, keeping him in sight, but staying between him and the surface. The four cetaceans arrowed toward the surface and grabbed a gulp of air, then settled back down, playfully cycling between Alex and Margo, gently jostling them. About thirty minutes later, Alex motioned Margo to join him. She released a bubble of air from her bag and dropped down beside him. Her console showed a depth of fifty meters. Alex pointed to a five-centimeter rip in the bottom curve of the tube's fluorescent covering.

Margo reached into a deep pocket located on the left leg of her suit and withdrew a roll of patching tape. Alex stretched the edges of the tear, and Margo applied a strip of self-sealing tape along the opening. Then she located a small pneumatic valve on the top of the tube and attached a hose from her spare air tank. On a signal from Alex, she released air into the tube, forcing water out through a one-way valve on the underside. She stopped when bubbles escaped from the lower valve.

As the tube rose slowly, Margo held on, keeping track of their progress on her console. They stopped rising when the gauge read thirty meters. Margo felt the tube—it was taut and solid. She tapped the back of her console, listening for the faint rush of sound in her ears. Nothing. She pointed to the back of her console and then her ear, and shook her head. Alex offered another of his exaggerated underwater shrugs and grinned, although the only part of the grin she could see was his crinkled eyes. She grinned back and pointed toward the suspension buoy and their boat, making an angled upward sign with her free hand. Alex nodded, checked his console, and they both headed back, slowly rising as they swam.

Margo saw Alex check his console from time to time, making certain they kept below the ever-changing ceiling limit it calculated for him. Since she had remained shallower than Alex for most of the dive, she knew she would be safe following his lead. She looked around at the four dolphins. Her earlier fright was gone, and she simply enjoyed George's protective nearness and the playful bumps and nudges from the others.

On the surface finally, Alex dropped his facemask down around his neck, fully inflated his bag, and grinned at Margo. "Close call down there!"

Margo shoved her facemask down and patted the glistening snout that appeared in front of her. "Thanks, George. I love you too."

The dolphin mewed a pleased response, lifted his body out of the water, and backed away, chattering as he went. The other three animals circled at and below the surface, keeping watch over their human charges.

"What happened to the EFCom?" Margo asked. "I expected it to come back online as soon as the antenna surfaced."

"Broken antenna wire, I imagine," Alex answered.

"Storm damage, I'm sure," said Margo, as they turned and headed toward the waiting vessel.

"Probably," agreed Alex. "But that wasn't a burst seam," he added.

"Yeah, maybe the sinking tube snapped the wire."

Actually, tube flotation chambers flooded on a regular basis. They had patched a full ten percent of them since the project started. But it was a bit unusual to find a rip on the tube bottom, and the Electrostatic Field Communication ("EFCom") transceivers on the buoys almost always survived.

※

The EFCom buoy nearest the tear had ceased transmitting, and the buoys on either side of the tear had signaled their departure from datum a day earlier. Alex had opted to employ an electrostatic field communication system, because of its clear underwater signal transmission capability that was independent of acoustic conditions, since it didn't rely on sound transmission through the water. Every buoy, each skimmer and floater, and every diver was outfitted with one of the small EFCom transceivers. Alex had inspected the non-transmitting buoy personally during an overflight from Jarvis Island. There was nothing visible on the two kilometers of surface between the buoys; they were closer together, but not so that it was visible to the eye. Nevertheless, the remaining 1,828-odd buoy-suspended kilometers of tube were stressing from the downward pull of the waterlogged section. The buoy near the tear was several meters underwater.

Suspended inside the flotation tube were two virtually impervious, lightweight, hose-like tubes, each about six centimeters in diameter, called vacuum sheaths. Two shallow channels jutted out from the bottom of each vacuum sheath, filled with electronically-controlled suspending magnets. Magnetically suspended inside each vacuum sheath was a five-centimeter tube of segmented soft iron officially called the rotor, but more popularly known as the ribbon, so named from the earliest conceptions back in the 1980s of the Launch Loop inventor, Keith Lofstrom. Alex was eager to check continuity readings to make certain the vacuum sheaths had not breached. They were not yet evacuated, but seawater entry at this stage would seriously delay the entire project. If the EFCom had not crapped out, the tests would already be underway.

Alex glanced ahead at Margo Jackson, cavorting with her four dolphins as they made their leisurely way back to the waiting boat. His field engineer in charge of underwater construction was a remarkable female. Nearly as tall as his own 183 centimeters, her model's slender figure, encased in electric-blue nylon-covered neoprene, seemed to lack feminine curves. He knew differently, of course, having joined her bikini-clad person from time to time for morning swims since the project began over two years ago.

The project—Alex had lived with it for three years before actual construction began. Longer, actually, if you considered dreams—since before the incredible, worldwide bi-millennial celebration when he still was a young boy.

There was the nearly simultaneous publication in America and England of practically identical ideas in 1985. Paul Birch published an article in *The Journal of the British Interplanetary Society*, while in America, Keith Lofstrom published his article in a supplement to *The Journal of the Astronautical Sciences*, he recalled. Nobody could agree on the names: Skyrail, Launch Loop, Beanstalk. There were others, but the idea is what counted, the sky-shaking idea that you don't need rockets to get into space.

Newspapers were full of explanations three-and-a-half years ago when the aging president of a computer software giant made the announcement. He would funnel a significant portion of company profits into the consortium. Space travel would become as commonplace and inexpensive as the personal computers his pioneering work had made possible. He went on to outline the easy-to-understand concept.

Imagine a water hose streaming water in a parabolic arch. Deflect the water and funnel it back to the start through a pump, creating a closed system. Make the stream strong enough and the hose light enough, and the entire structure will support itself—the water holding up the hose structure. Now, replace the water with a thin, closed-loop pipe of segmented soft iron. Make it 5,000 kilometers around and accelerate it to orbital velocity with gigantic linear induction motors from two points on the equator 2,000 kilometers apart. The center section of the structure, including both the outgoing and return legs of the loop, will rise to about eighty kilometers above the Earth. Supply access to the upstream end in space with a Kevlar-hung elevator, and you can launch capsules by magnetically coupling them to the rapidly moving pipe of iron.

Slingshot, they called it. The greatest engineering undertaking in the history of the world, they said.

As the on-scene project manager, Alex was responsible for getting the job done, on schedule, on budget. He was building a gossamer structure over 2,500 kilometers long, a frail spider web, completely invisible when viewed from more than a few kilometers. Alex grinned wryly. All *Slingshot* really consisted of was a fancy evacuated tube, a flexible iron pipe, four linear drivers and their power sources, some guy wires, and a couple of elevators. Put that way, it seemed simple enough. But, of course, it wasn't simple at all, and for all his skill and engineering competence, and despite surface appearances, deep down Alex was not entirely sure that he could make it happen.

Margo and Alex climbed up the ladder and onto *Skimmer One's* bobbing fantail. This was one of two skimmers on the project—twelve-meter-long surface-effect boats that looked more like a floating aircraft than a traditional motorboat. They were capable of 200 knots, skimming about one-and-a-half meters over the wave tops. They had a small open fantail, just large enough for a couple of divers to doff their gear. Being on the fantail when the skimmer was on its cushion was more than dangerous, and was strictly prohibited throughout the project.

Alex signaled to the waiting coxswain, and they got underway for Baker, plowing through the water while Alex and Margo remained exposed. He and Margo stood near the stern railing and removed their dripping skins. Alex looked back at the buoys, now presumably in their proper places.

"How many more times?" Alex looked quizzically at Margo.

"Who knows?" She glanced back at the bobbing buoys. "We have repair people available at both ends. We shouldn't be doing this ourselves, you know." She turned and looked directly at Alex. "What do you think—weather or sabotage?"

Alex shrugged and tossed the spent carbon dioxide cartridge from his shark stick in the general direction of the cavorting dolphins. "I wanted to see for myself, and I still don't know. Does it matter? We can't patrol the entire eighteen-hundred-twenty-eight-kilometer length anyway."

"What are we dealing with?" Margo asked. "You don't get out here in a rowboat."

"We're two thousand wet klicks from any kind of civilization," Alex said. "At minimum, that's a large motor-yacht or even an ocean sailer—you know, one of those we maybe can afford when this job is done." He sighed. "We're dealing with lots of money and someone with a major bitch."

He looked into her green eyes.

"Just keep my tubes at depth." His blue eyes flashed, and he turned toward the cockpit to radio his orders to test pipe continuity.

※

Margo dropped her eyes at his challenge. For the thousandth time, she asked herself if she had bitten off more than she could chew with this assignment. Was it her fault that the flotation chambers kept ripping? Was she missing something important? Was she copping out to imply there might have been sabotage? And yet, Alex seemed to agree that it might be sabotage. When she joined the project two years ago, the newspapers had acclaimed her as the ideal role model for the new twenty-first-century woman. At times that burden lay heavily on her shoulders, as it did now, she reflected.

It was a vast responsibility, and there was no way one person actually could control all of it at once. How Alex handled the weight of the entire project awed her, but she was careful never to let him know.

Margo watched Alex step into the cockpit. He was tall and slender, richly tanned from his constant outdoor work. She felt a softness well up inside her, a gentle warmth spreading out from the pit of her stomach. She bit her lower lip and turned angrily to lean on the after-railing.

None of that, she chided herself. This assignment was too important, and the stakes too high, to let any kind of emotion intrude. As she entered the cabin and sealed the port, the skipper switched modes, and pressurized air quickly filled the hard-sided skirt. In moments the skimmer lifted out of the water, except for the port and starboard skirts that protruded about a meter into the waves. Within seconds, high-pressure water nozzles jetted water from the end of each skirt, and within thirty seconds, *Skimmer One* was approaching 200 knots.

As *Skimmer One* headed into the afternoon sun, trailing an arrow-straight wake of white foam, Margo stood looking aft through the sealed port, remembering her instinctive sharing, and their underwater kiss following the fright of nearly becoming shark food. She shook off the sensation and busied herself with putting away their diving equipment. But a hint of a smile remained on her lips as they shot over the surface, finally settling back onto the water as they entered the small protected artificial harbor on the west side of Baker Island, just south of a shallow reef that went dry at low tide.

You have just been reading from Chapter One of Slingshot,
*the 1st book in **The Starchild** Trilogy, Robert Williscroft's*
exciting Science Fiction trilogy.

To read the rest of this book,
click here: Slingshot.

WORDS OF PRAISE FOR SLINGSHOT

Slingshot does for the launch loop what Arthur C. Clarke's *The Fountains of Paradise* or Sheffield's *Web Between the Worlds* did for the space elevator. Again, Williscroft delivers a great mix of hard science fiction and action.

— **Alastair Mayer**
Author of the T-Space Series

Robert Williscroft deftly crafts an energetic story around a phenomenal technological development just over the horizon: the space launch loop. The technical detail woven into this story is an education unto itself. But don't assume that Williscroft chooses raw infodump over story—*Slingshot* is an adventure that pulls you in, gives you characters that are engaging, and invites you to follow them through their challenges. What Williscroft has done in *Slingshot* is no easy task—he has balanced the *hard* aspect of science fiction with the character portrayals that those who despise that very *hard* science fiction beg for. The last decade has seen impressive leaps in the theoretical work toward the launch loop—this book couldn't come too soon! And you won't be able to keep from reading all the way to the end. Williscroft's art continues to be praise-worthy!

— **Jason D. Batt**, *100 Year Starship*
Author of *The Tales of Dreamside* series

I've been a fan of Robert Williscroft's books for a while now. They're action-packed and filled with all kinds of interesting, real-world information. *Slingshot* fits right in.

Slingshot is about the development of an earth-bound spaceport in which spaceships are taken 80 kilometers above the Earth by elevator and hurled onto their trajectory by a very fast-moving ribbon of soft iron. It is much easier, cheaper, and cleaner to launch spaceships from here due to the rarified atmosphere. This concept may be a reality someday. The book begins with a foreword by Keith Lofstrom, the originator of this concept called the "launch loop."

Learning about the launch loop is the most interesting aspect of this novel. Williscroft's descriptions of the construction techniques, its operations, and the benefits for space travel are absolutely fascinating. The book takes place about thirty years in the future, and I could easily see such a project becoming a reality in that time.

The plot of the novel is driven by the development and construction of the project, which is being threatened by ill-informed environmentalists bent on destroying the project. The launch loop is far greener than the current method of launching vehicles into space, but a sinister power has misled the environmentalists into believing that sabotaging the launch loop is saving the planet. Meanwhile, the sinister power is protecting its own economic interests.

As usual, Williscroft has created a cast of interesting and driven characters. The book is a fascinating read, and you are guaranteed not only to learn a lot, but to dream about the future of space travel.

Marc Weitz, Past President
The Los Angeles Adventurers' Club

Click here to read Slingshot

ABOUT THE AUTHOR

Dr. Robert G. Williscroft served twenty-three years in the U.S. Navy and the National Oceanic and Atmospheric Administration (NOAA). He commenced his service as an enlisted nuclear Submarine Sonar Technician in 1961, was selected for the Navy Enlisted Scientific Education Program in 1966, and graduated from University of Washington in Marine Physics and Meteorology in 1969. He returned to nuclear submarines as the Navy's first Poseidon Weapons Officer. Subsequently, he served as Navigator and Diving Officer on both catamaran mother vessels for the Deep Submergence Rescue Vehicle. Then he joined the Submarine Development Group One out of San Diego as the Officer-in-Charge of the Test Operations Group, conducting "deep-ocean surveillance and data acquisition"—which forms the basis for his Cold War novel *Operation Ivy Bells: A Mac McDowell Mission*.

In NOAA Dr. Williscroft directed diving operations throughout the Pacific and Atlantic. As a certified diving instructor for both the National Association of Underwater Instructors (NAUI) and the Multinational Diving Educators Association (MDEA), he taught over 3,000 individuals both basic and advanced SCUBA diving. He authored four diving books, developed the first NAUI drysuit course, developed advanced curricula for mixed gas and other specialized diving modes, and developed and taught a NAUI course on the Math and Physics of Advanced Diving. His doctoral dissertation for California Coast University, *A System for Protecting SCUBA Divers from the Hazards of Contaminated Water* was published by the U.S.

Department of Commerce and distributed to Port Captains worldwide. He also served three shipboard years in the high Arctic conducting scientific baseline studies, and thirteen months at the geographic South Pole in charge of National Science Foundation atmospheric projects.

Dr. Williscroft has written extensively on terrorism and related subjects. He is the author of a popular book on current events published by Pelican Publishing: *The Chicken Little Agenda—Debunking Experts' Lies*, now in its second edition as an eBook, and a new children's book series, *Starman Jones*, in collaboration with Dr. Frank Drake, world-famous director of the Carl Sagan Center for the Study of Life in the Universe and the SETI Institute.

Dr. Williscroft's 1st novel in *The Starchild Trilogy*, *Slingshot*, tells the story of the construction of the world's first Space Launch Loop. *Slingshot* was launched at the Seattle International Space Elevator Conference in August 2015. His 2nd novel in *The Starchild Trilogy, The Starchild Compact,* is based on the discovery that Saturn's moon Iapetus is actually a derelict starship, and how Earth explorers eventually meet with the "Founders," who originally arrived on the starship and populated the Earth long ago. In the 3rd book in *The Starchild Trilogy, The Iapetus Federation*, the Federation expands Solar Systemwide, while a new Caliphate sweeps Earth. The Starchild Institute creates wormhole portals to enable the Exodus. Earth becomes medieval, while human focus shifts to the Iapetus Federation. Humans settle every potentially habitable spot in the Solar System and begin expanding into the rest of the Galaxy.

Dr. Williscroft's most recent novel, *Icicle—A Tensor Matrix*, is a hard science fiction story about a wealthy engineer in today's world who has terminal cancer and arranges for his head to be cryonically preserved. He wakes up about a century later inside an electronic matrix. He becomes the spearhead of humanity's defensive effort against an invading space fleet operating under the Dark Forest Theory (Like hunters in a "dark forest," a civilization can never be certain of an alien civilization's true intentions. The extreme distances between stars creates an insurmountable "chain of suspicion," where any two civilizations cannot communicate well enough to dissipate mistrust, making conflict inevitable.) This is the first of three books in *The Oort Chronicles*.

Dr. Williscroft is an active member of the Colorado Author's League, Science Fiction Writers of America, Libertarian Futurist Society, Los Angeles Adventurers' Club, Mensa, Military Officer's Association, American Legion, and NRA. He lives in Centennial, Colorado, with his wife, Jill, and their twin college boys (when they are home from school).

OTHER WORKS BY ROBERT G. WILLISCROFT

Please visit Amazon.com to discover other eBooks by Robert Williscroft and your favorite online or Brick & Mortar bookseller for their paper versions:

Current events:

The Chicken Little Agenda—Debunking "Experts'" Lies

Children's books:

The Starman Jones Series:
    Starman Jones: A Relativity Birthday Present
    Starman Jones Goes to the Dogs (scheduled for release in 2020)

Short Stories:

The Daedalus Files:
Daedalus
Daedalus—LEO
Daedalus—Squad
Daedalus—Combat

Novels:

Mac McDowell Missions:
    Operation Ivy Bells
    Operation Snow Cone (Scheduled for release 2020)

The Starchild Trilogy:
   Slingshot
   The Starchild Compact
   The Iapetus Federation
The Daedalus Files
The Oort Chronicles:
   Icicle—A Tensor Matrix (scheduled for release in 2020)
   The Oort—Interstellar Consequences (scheduled for release in 2020)
   Oort Andromeda—Galactic Diaspora (scheduled for release in 2021)

CONNECT WITH ROBERT G. WILLISCROFT

I really appreciate you reading my book! Here are my social media coordinates:

Friend me on Facebook: *https://www.facebook.com/robert.williscroft*

Follow me on Twitter: *@RGWilliscroft*

Like my Amazon author page: *https://www.amazon.com/Robert-G.-Williscroft/e/B001JP52AS*

Subscribe to my blog: *https://thrawnrickle.com/*

Connect on LinkedIn: *https://www.linkedin.com/in/argee/*

Visit my book website: *https://robertwilliscroft.com*

Visit my personal website: *https://argee.net*

THE DAEDALUS FILES GLOSSARY

AFRICOM—American centralized military command and control for the African continent.
Atoll—A ring-shaped reef, island, or chain of islands formed of coral.
Baker Compound—The *Slingshot* facility on Baker Island.
BatCap—Power source for the Pulsed Energy Weapon, a unique marriage of a 3-D battery and a thin, large-surface-area flexible capacitor that the SWIC member wears on his back. The capacitor supports twenty rapid-release lethal laser bursts and recharges in less than a minute from the 3-D battery, or it can continuously support a lethal laser burst every five seconds. The 3-D battery needs recharging every five thousand bursts.
BUDS—Basic Underwater Demolition/SEAL training.
CS Platypus—*Cruise Ship Platypus*
Cumulonimbus calvus—A moderately tall cumulonimbus cloud which is capable of precipitation, but has not yet reached the tropopause.
Cumulonimbus cloud—Thunderhead cloud.
CYA—Cover your ass.
Deflector—A series of permanent and electro-magnets that bend the path of the rapidly moving iron ribbon.
EMT—Emergency Medical Technician.
ETA—Estimated time of arrival.
Fulton—A surface-to-air extraction system developed in the 1950s. It involves using a harness and a self-inflating balloon with an attached

lift line. A C-130-type aircraft engages the line with a V-shaped yoke on its nose, and the person is reeled on board.

Gryphon-7—A wingsuit-like carapace strapped on the body. It stopped short of the feet, but in flight could extend to a full two meters, stretching beyond the feet. It attached to the legs and arms, with special controls for each hand, and had a broad Velcro band across the midriff. It had extensible delta wings with a three-meter wingspan. The back end contained a small steerable hypergolic rocket engine, and the left and right wings each contained pressurized hypergolic fuel components. Switches in the hand units controlled the fuel valves. The *Gryphon* had a heads-up display with height-over-ground, airspeed, groundspeed, compass, and GPS coordinates superimposed on a map, plus various system readouts.

Gryphon-10—Like *Gryphon-7* with some radical changes including full body armor with circulating fuel for heat protection, an increased surface area using dimples, wrinkles, and rolls that dramatically boosted heat shedding, and it incorporated a new type of polymer that was stronger, lighter, and more heat resistant than anything before. The biggest change was Mother, the guidance computer unit designed to act on its calculations before the human pilot was even aware of them. Still man-transportable, although more ungainly than *Gryphon-7*. Its unpowered glide ratio was 14-1, and it could fly 100 level klicks under power.

Gryphon-10, Mk 4—Looked exactly like the *Gryphon-10*. It differed in subtle ways because of improvements developed during several LEO drops. Incorporated the latest model of a very efficient, hand-held, pulsed energy weapon into a node in the leading edge of either the left or right wing. Its power source is a lightweight BatCap. Before opening the carapace after landing, the SWIC member retrieves the weapon from its node and holsters it just like a sidearm.

Gryphon-10, Mk 5—Exactly like the *Gryphon-10, Mk 4*, except for the addition of a rear-firing pulsed energy weapon.

Howland Island—A coral island in the equatorial Pacific about sixty-five kilometers north of Baker Island. It was the destination of Amelia Earhart when she disappeared.

HP oxygen—High-pressure oxygen

Hypergolic fuel—Fuel that ignites spontaneously when the individual fuel elements come into contact.

Hypergolic rocket or jet—A rocket or jet that uses hypergolic fuel.

Jarvis Compound—The *Slingshot* facility on Jarvis Island.

Keith Lofstrom—Inventor of the Launch Loop.

Kick thruster—A small, reigniteable solid-state rocket attached to a capsule, used for vector changes after release from the rail, or to slow down a capsule used to transit from Baker to Jarvis.

Klick—Slang word for kilometer.

Launch Loop—A means for getting into space without using rockets.

Launch Loop International—The company that and manages Slingshot.

Launch pouch—Attaches to the capsule underside, enabling magnetic acceleration of the capsule by the rail.

LEO—Low Earth Orbit

Mach number—The ratio of the speed of a body to the speed of sound in the surrounding medium.

Maglev train—A magnetically levitated train; it floats above the track propelled by magnetism.

Mayotte Island—A small island northwest of Madagascar that has the largest coral-reef enclosed lagoon of any island in the world.

MOS—Military Occupation Specialty

Pallet—A regular cargo pallet used to transport cargo up the Skytower and along the rail for launch into orbit. Each pallet carried four tanks. Two were HP oxygen used by the flyer until Gryphon separation, attached to the wingsuit with breakaway connectors. The other two carried hypergolic fuel, UDMH and nitrogen tetroxide, for the small hypergolic maneuvering jets

Pulsed Energy Weapon—Fires pulsed high-energy laser bursts. Is virtually silent.

Rail—Common term for the portion of the launch loop between the skyports.

Ribbon—Common term for the soft-iron tube that is the heart of the launch loop.

SEAL—An acronym for *Sea Air and Land*; a member of a Naval Special Warfare unit trained for unconventional warfare.

Skyport—The structure at the top of the skytower.

Skyrail—An alternative name for a Space Elevator or Launch Loop.

Skytower—The elevator-like set of cables that extends from the Skyport to the island below.

Slingshot—The Space Launch Loop between Baker and Jarvis Islands in the equatorial Pacific.

Socket—The attachment point on the island for the skytower.

SPELCO—Special Parachute and Logistics Consortium

Stratosphere—The second major layer of Earth's atmosphere, just above the troposphere.

Suspensor cable—A cable to which the skytower cable and double-lift cables are attached. It carries the weight of all the cables.

SWIC—SEAL Winged Insertion Command

Tensioner—A cable attached to the rail or downslopes and the ocean bottom, with a dynamic device that increases or decreases the tension as necessary to maintain Launch Loop stability.

Tropopause—The interface between the troposphere and the stratosphere.

Troposphere—The lowest region of the atmosphere, extending from the earth's surface to a height of about 6–10 km, which is the lower boundary of the stratosphere.

UDMH—Unsymmetrical dimethylhydrazine, a hypergolic fuel component (see nitrogen tetroxide).

UV light—Ultraviolet light.

Wingsuit—Aa suit with fabric filling the gaps between stretched out arms and ankles, and between the legs, enabling the wearer to glide through the air.

Fresh Ink Group
Independent Multi-media Publisher
Fresh Ink Group / Push Pull Press

☙

Hardcovers
Softcovers
All Ebook Platforms
Audiobooks
Worldwide Distribution

☙

Indie Author Services
Book Development, Editing, Proofing
Graphic/Cover Design
Video/Trailer Production
Website Creation
Social Media Management
Writing Contests
Writers' Blogs
Podcasts

☙

Authors
Editors
Artists
Experts
Professionals

☙

FreshInkGroup.com
info@FreshInkGroup.com
Twitter: @FreshInkGroup
Facebook.com/FreshInkGroup
LinkedIn: Fresh Ink Group

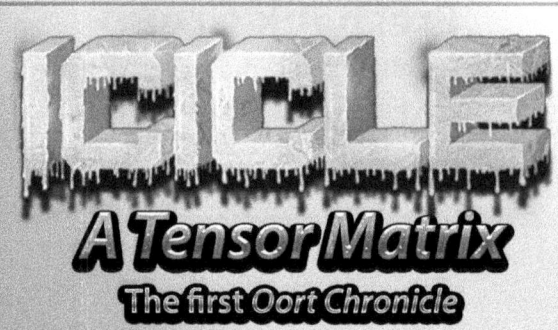

Saturation Dive Team Officer-in-Charge (OIC) Mac McDowell faces his greatest challenge yet, leading the team into a critical Cold War mission. With a security clearance above Top Secret, Mac and his off-the-books deep-water espionage group must gather Russian intel to avert world war. Join nuclear-submariner Mac as he extreme-dives to a thousand feet, battles giant squids, and proves what brave men can achieve under real pressure, the kind that will steal your air and crush the life out of you. *Operation Ivy Bells: A Mac McDowell Mission* updates the popular bestseller by Robert G. Williscroft, a lifelong adventurer who blends his own experiences with real events to craft a military thriller that will take your breath away. **Fresh Ink** Group

Milton Keynes UK
Ingram Content Group UK Ltd.
UKHW010226080224
437388UK00001B/3/J